喚醒你的英文語感！

Get a Feel for English !

喚醒你的英文語感！

Get a Feel for English !

搞定商務口說

Oral Business Communication

總編審 / 王復國

作者 / Dana Forsythe

PREFACE

Oral communication in business situations is different than oral communication for general conversation. Oral business communication is specialized and a little more formal. People who use English for business need to know this specialized and more formal English, if they are to communicate successfully. Doing business is all about good communication, so knowing the correct English means making profitable business deals!

Oral business communication is specialized, but it is not really complex. You can master this style of communication if you study it and practice it. This book provides the knowledge and skills that you must have in order to communicate successfully in business situations. I am sure you will find the organization of the language material logical and easy to follow.

Finally, here is a book that 1) contains no insignificant material such as low use vocabulary and expressions, and 2) provides the most important language for the most common business situations. The material presented here is comprehensive, and it also has innovations that will make your learning even better.

May this book help you—and your company—complete many successful business deals!

Dana Forsythe

　　商場上的口語溝通不同於一般會話。商業的口語溝通屬於專門性的對話，而且稍微比較正式。以英語洽商的人士若要成功地溝通，便需了解這些專業、以及較為正式的用語。談生意的關鍵在於良好的溝通，所以了解正確的英文用語意謂著談成獲利豐厚的生意！

　　口語商業溝通雖然專業，但其實並不複雜。如果各位經過研讀和練習，也可以精通這種溝通的方式。本書提供各位在商場上成功溝通不可不知的知識與技巧。我確信各位會覺得這些用語資料的編排不但切合邏輯，而且易於遵循。

　　最後要說的是，這本書 1) 所提供的資料都是最重要的、使用度最高的字彙和表達方式，2)為最常見的商業情境提供最重要的用語。在此提供的資料不但範圍廣泛，且具創意，能讓各位的學習效果更上一層樓。

　　希望本書能協助各位──以及各位的公司──在商場上無往不利！

Dana Forsythe

推薦序

　　台灣因加入 WTO，產業國際化的速度加快，使英文能力成為職場上每一個人必備的核心能力。由於職務關係，使我更能深刻體會，在競爭激烈的國際商戰中，英文能力也是一項必備的武器，能有效而正確的運用英文，不但能縮短與國際客戶的距離，更是為組織及個人建立專業形象的第一步。

　　對於英語學習，我一向認為沒有什麼秘訣，勤能補拙，培養學習興趣是最可靠的方式，雖然工作多年以來，使用英文的機會頻繁，但也曾為了如何運用更專業的英文，花費不少心力學習，直到 2000 年間，在一次短期的學習機緣中，接受了 Dana 的專業指導，使我的英語能力更上層樓，同時也讓我深切的認知，透過好的老師及專業的教材，也是掌握英語學習方法、建立英語學習成就感的首要之道！

　　很高興 Dana 終於要出書了，這本書把他的教學經驗用更有效的方法傳遞出去。同樣令我興奮的是，當我閱畢這本書後，得到更多於當年接受短期指導以外的東西。在不同商場情境下，除可以運用專業正確的英文進行溝通外，進而能學習培養自己的英文溝通風格。個人認為這本書對於一個每天必需倚賴英文從事專業工作的人來說，不但實用，更能夠在英語自學中建立學習成就感。這也是這本書重要的特點。

廖經民

策略行銷處經理

臺灣積體電路製造公司

　　WTO 的時代已來臨，公司國際化的腳步愈來愈快，與外國客戶「談」生意已是無法避免的情況，於是乎能以英文溝通變成了馳騁商場必備的籌碼。本書正是順應這個需求而產生。書中囊括了商場上最常見的情境，從與客戶會面、接待客戶，進而與其開會、談判……等，讀者該怎麼說、怎麼答，本書皆有完整的介紹。另作者依其跨文化的觀察及在台教授商務英文多年之經驗，在書中提醒與西方人言商時應注意的事項，也列舉出國人開口說英文時易犯的錯誤，以供讀者作為參考、借鏡。

　　為建立讀者學習的信心，本書內容從字彙、例句乃至對話，由簡而繁、深入淺出，引導讀者循序漸進的學習，不致輕言放棄。本書另附有 CD，完整收錄書中字彙、例句及對話，讓讀者反覆聆聽，自然習慣英文發音和語調，克服開口說英文的心理障礙，有效打造口說實力。

本書將介紹各位在以英文洽商時所有必備的基本語言技能。研讀本書之後，各位在一般洽商情境中，對於和西方商業人士溝通所需的核心英語能力會更有自信。

本書主要特色

BIZ 必通字彙、片語、句型

要想純熟地運用商用英文，本書介紹的英文字彙、片語、以及句型，都是各位必須知道的。這些必備的商用英文大多出現在標示「BIZ必通字彙 / 片語 / 句型」的單元內。在單元內（或緊接其後）則舉例說明如何使用這些字彙、片語以及句型。

豐富的範例

本書各個章節都有許多的範例。經驗豐富的語言教師都知道，不論是教授哪種語言，最常聽到的問題就是：「你可以舉一個例子嗎？」語言學習者需要豐富的範例，才能了解如何運用新的字彙、片語以及句型。本書提供了大量的例子，讓各位充分了解每個詞句的使用方法。

糾正錯誤

排除錯誤，想當然爾，是精通新語言的過程中重要的環節。本書各章節都會有「小心陷阱」的說明，如下圖所示，說明中國人說英語時常犯的錯誤。

```
┌┄┄┄┄┄┄┄┄┄┄┄┄◇◇◇ 小心陷阱 ◇◇◇┄┄┄┄┄┄┄┄┄┄┄┐
┊ ☹ 錯誤用法                                          ┊
┊   This is Jane **call** from Lion Coffee Makers.    ┊
┊ ☺ 正確用法                                          ┊
┊   This is Jane **calling** from Lion Coffee Makers. ┊
└┄┄┄┄┄┄┄┄┄┄┄┄┄┄┄┄┄┄┄┄┄┄┄┄┄┄┄┄┄┄┄┄┄┄┄┄┄┄┘
```

實戰演練

　　學習英語的學生必須透過練習，才能將新學到的技巧靈活運用到真實生活當中。本書每一章都有練習活動，而這些活動是針對兩人以上的練習設計的。「實戰演練」中的練習是協助各位加強商用英文熟練度非常實用的獨特方法。

如何使用本書

　　本書使用方法簡單。只要逐步閱讀每個章節，並配合「實戰演練」練習，就能充分培養出你的技巧。強烈建議各位高聲朗誦，讓這些句子更深刻地烙印在大腦的語言處理中樞。

「I」和「We」

　　「I」（我）這個字在本書的用法說明以及範例中出現的次數很多。在許多或大多數的情況下，其實可以使用「We」（我們）這個字來代替「I」。不過，為了簡化起見，書中只用「I」，而不是「I/We」。

輕鬆複習

　　回頭溫習本書各章節商業英文用語的方法很簡單。只要針對「BIZ必通字彙／片語／句型」和「Show Time」的單元反覆練習即可。

實戰演練

　　實戰演練是針對兩人一組設計的活動：A員以及B員。因此，你必

須找一位夥伴一同練習。你也可以找多位夥伴。如果你的夥伴不只一位，多出的一人或多人可以扮演監督者的角色。以下所示即為如何組織練習的建議。

2人一組	A員	B員

3人一組	A員	B員
	監督者	

4人一組	A員兩名	B員兩名
	或	
	A員	B員
	A監督者	B監督者

5人一組	A員兩名	B員兩名
	監督者	

CONTENTS

第二部分 Section TWO
正式溝通的模式 Formal Communication Formats

第四章 打電話 Telephoning

第七章 談判 Negotiations

第八章　介紹自己的公司 Presenting Your Company

ONE

人際溝通

Relationship Communication

　　與外國人做生意，不論在事前或事後，我們都得打好關係。第一部分涵蓋了進行有效的人際溝通時，所需的所有英語基本元素。

　　Before and after we do business with foreigners, we engage in relationship building. This section covers all of the basic English language components that you need in order to engage in effective relationship communication.

第 1 章

與他人會面
Meeting People

「會面」是建立良好商務關係的第一步。你必須先把關係打好，接著才能進行生意往來。本章即在介紹建立商務關係的第一步時，你所必備的用語。

Meeting people is the beginning of building good business relationships. Before you can do business, you must establish a relationship. This chapter will give you the English you need to start the relationship-building process.

1 認人 Identifying People

　　有時候你得和素未謀面的人見面，在這樣的情況下，你必須先認出這個（些）人。例如，你到機場接機，或是在擠滿人的會議室裡與某個人見面，你就得先確認這個人是否為你要見的對象。如果認錯人，你很可能會對著不相干的人自我介紹一番，這樣可就糗大了！

★★★ *BIZ 一點通* ★★★

「Meet」的解釋有兩種！一個意思是：第一次與某人認識。

例 Hi, Joe, I don't think we have met before. I am Jill Simmons.

嗨，喬，我想我們以前沒見過吧。我是吉爾‧西蒙。

另一個意思則是：兩個或兩個以上原本就相識的人約在某處見面。

例 I am going to meet my husband at the movie theater after work.

我下班後要去電影院和我先生碰面。

BIZ 必通句型

❶ ARE YOU...?

請問你是……嗎？

例 Pardon me. Are you Mr. Burk?

對不起，請問你是柏克先生嗎？

例 Hello. Are you Ms. Livingston of Salt Lake Computers?

哈囉，請問你是鹽湖電腦的李文斯頓女士嗎？

❷ YOU MUST BE...

你一定就是……

例 Hi! You must be Robert Johnson.

嗨！你一定就是羅伯‧強生了。

❸ **YOU ARE..., AREN'T YOU?**

你是……，對不對？

例 Excuse me. You are Julia Roberts, aren't you?

對不起，你是茱莉亞‧蘿伯茲，對不對？

❹ **COULD YOU BE...BY ANY CHANCE?**

你會不會就是……？

例 Could you be Miss Warner, by any chance?

請問你是不是就是華納小姐？

　　本書提供許多同義的範例。就如上方「BIZ 必通句型」，這四個句型都是教你在認人時應該如何措詞。如果你覺得要記住所有的例句很困難，不妨試試這個方法：挑一兩個你比較喜歡的例句，然後記起來，並且反覆大聲背頌，讓它深植腦海中。這麼一來，這個句子就會成爲你自己的。當你需要的時候，自然就會脫口而出。

　　這是個非常重要的原則，本書稍後還會不斷地提醒各位讀者。

★★★ BIZ 一點通 ★★★

如果你到機場接機，通常應該詢問對方：How was your flight? （這趟飛行還順利嗎？）

2 介紹 Introduction

　　介紹的技巧很重要：不論是自我介紹、還是介紹別人彼此認識皆是如此。第一印象很重要，如果你在介紹的時候態度從容、友善，可因此提升自己的專業形象。

　　對很多不以英文爲母語的人來說，每當碰到一些必須以英文做介紹或是與新朋友交談的場合，往往會緊張不已。其實用不著這麼緊張。因爲介紹時說的客套話就好比套用數學公式一般。這部分將會介紹各位「介紹公式」中所需的用語。

　　記住，一定要反覆練習這些句子，直到你能自然地脫口而出爲止。

2.1 向他人自我介紹 Introducing Yourself to Another

　　當兩個社會地位不同的人第一次見面時，最好是由階級或是地位「較低者」向「較高者」做自我介紹。例如，如果你到對方公司拜訪，由於洽商地點在對方公司，他的「地位」就應視爲比你的高。因此，你應該採取主動：向對方自我介紹。

　　自我介紹時，請告知對方你的姓名、職稱以及所屬公司。

BIZ 必通句型

❶ **I AM..., THE...OF/FOR/AT/IN...**

我是……，……公司的……

例 Hello. I am Josh McDowell, the General Manager of 7-11 in the U.S.

哈囉，我是喬許・麥道威，美國 7-11 的總經理。

例 Hi. I am Jill Steinbrenner, a photographer for *National Geographic* magazine.

你好，我是吉爾・史坦布蘭納，國家地理雜誌攝影師。

例 Hello. I am President Tsai's Executive Assistant at Hsinchu Machines.
哈囉，我是新竹機械公司蔡董的執行助理。

❷ ALLOW ME TO INTRODUCE MYSELF. I AM...
請容我自我介紹，我是……
例 Allow me to introduce myself. I am Jenny Bridges. I work for ABC Company.
請容我自我介紹，我是珍妮・布利基，我在 ABC 公司工作。

❸ LET ME INTRODUCE MYSELF. I AM...
容我自我介紹，我是……
例 Let me introduce myself. I am Cliff Broland.
讓我自我介紹一下，我是克利夫・布洛藍。

❹ I DON'T THINK WE HAVE MET BEFORE. I AM...
我想我們以前沒見過，我是……
例 I don't think we have met before. I am Betty Windam.
我想我們以前沒見過，我是貝蒂・溫頓。

❺ NICE TO MEET YOU.
很高興認識你。
（這句可以作為自我介紹的結語）
例 I am Vince Foster of Washington Wafers. Nice to meet you.
我是華盛頓晶圓公司的文斯・福斯特。很高興認識你。

Word list

geographic〔͵dʒɪə`græfɪk〕 *adj.* 地理的　　　　　wafer〔`wefɚ〕 *n.* 晶圓

❻ PLEASED TO MEET YOU.

很高興認識你。

（這句可以作為自我介紹的結語）

例 I am Vicky Swanson. Pleased to meet you.

我是維琪・史文森。很高興認識你。

❼ IT'S A PLEASURE TO MEET YOU.

很高興認識你。

（這句可以作為自我介紹的結語）

例 I am Harriet Bookman. Pleased to meet you.

我是哈莉艾特・布克曼。很高興認識你。

◇◇◇ 小心陷阱 ◇◇◇

1 ☹ 錯誤用法

Allow me to **introducing** myself.

請容我自我介紹。

☺ 正確用法

Allow me to **introduce** myself.

請容我自我介紹。

2 ☹ 錯誤用法

Please to meet you.

很高興認識你。

☺ 正確用法

Pleased to meet you.

很高興認識你。

當別人對你作自我介紹，請如以下所示，將他們的措詞重複一遍：

"Nice to meet you, too."

"Pleased to meet you, too."

"It's a pleasure to meet you, too."

「我也很高興認識你。」

或者，你也可以這麼說：

"Me, too."

"Likewise."

「我也是。」

2.1a 向知曉但從未謀面的人自我介紹

Self-introduction to a Familiar Person

下列的例子中，A雖然知道B是何許人，但是從來不曾見過B。

Show Time

❶ A: Hi. Are you Julius Simpson?

B: Yes, I am.

A: Hi, I am Ally Cooby of the Louisiana Lawyers' Association. Nice to meet you.

B: Nice to meet you, too.

A: If you have a moment, I would like to ask you a question.

B: Sure.

A ：你好，請問你是朱利亞斯‧辛普森嗎？

B ：是的，我就是。

A ：你好，我是路易斯安那州律師協會的艾莉‧庫比。很高興認識你。

B ：我也很高興認識你。

Word list

association〔ə,sosɪ`eʃən〕 n. 協會；團體

A：如果您有空的話，我想請教一個問題。

B：沒問題。

② A: You must be Phyllis Savage.

B: Yes, I am.

A: Hi, I am Lawrence Oliver, the Marketing Manager of Taiwan Tobacco. I am here to give you a ride to your hotel.

B: Oh, great. Pleased to meet you.

A: Pleased to meet you, too.

A：你一定就是菲莉絲‧賽維區。

B：沒錯，我就是。

A：你好，我是勞倫斯‧奧利佛，台灣煙草公司的行銷經理。我是來接您到飯店的。

B：喔，太好了。很高興認識你。

A：我也很高興認識你。

2.1b 向陌生人自我介紹 Self-introduction to a Stranger

以下這些例子當中，A 並不認識 B。

Show Time

❶ A: Hi, I am Clarence Darrow, a salesman at Jiffy Jello.

B: Hello, I am Ruby Faulk, a telemarketer for Cowloon

Word list

tobacco〔təˋbæko〕 n. 煙草   telemarketer〔ˌtɛləˋmɑrkɪtɚ〕 n. 電話行銷人員

Clothiers.

A: It's a pleasure to meet you.

B: It's a pleasure to meet you, too.

A: This is a boring seminar, don't you think?

B: Oh, I think it's a little interesting, actually.

A：嗨，我是克萊倫斯‧戴羅，Jiffy Jello 的業務員。

B：哈囉，我是露比‧福克，Cowloon 成衣公司的電話行銷人員。

A：很高興認識你。

B：我也很高興認識你。

A：這個研討會挺無聊的，你不覺得嗎？

B：喔，其實，我覺得還蠻有趣的。

❷ A: Your meal smells good.

B: Yes, it is.

A: Allow me to introduce myself. I am Jeremy Bush of Michigan Machinery.

B: Hi, I am Pauline Tsai, a technician at Taiwan Business Machines.

A: Nice to meet you.

B: Likewise.

A：你的餐點好香啊。

B：是啊，的確很香。

A：容我自我介紹，我是密西根機械公司的傑瑞米‧布希。

B：嗨，我是蔡寶琳，台灣商業機器的技術員。

ord list

seminar〔ˋsɛməˌnɑr〕n. 研討會　　　technician〔tɛkˋnɪʃən〕n. 技術人員

A：很高興認識你。
B：我也是。

2.2 介紹人們認識彼此 Introducing People to Each Other

介紹人們認識彼此不像自我介紹這麼容易，不過還是有規則可循，只要遵循這套公式，就萬事OK了！

首先，必須牢記一個原則：將「地位較低者」介紹給「地位較高者」。在介紹的時候，先叫出地位較高者的稱謂。

要如何判定哪個人的地位較高呢？一般情況下，有以下幾個判斷方式：

★如果有人造訪你的公司，你公司員工的地位就比這個人來的高。

★如果是在非正式的場合，例如咖啡廳，外國訪客的地位就高於你的同事。不過，也許你會想要維護自己老闆或上司的地位，這就要視老闆隨和的程度而定了。

記住，介紹他人互相認識時需要提供姓名、職稱、所屬公司等資訊。不過也可以省略大家都知道的部分。例如，大家都知道彼此屬於哪家公司，就不必再加以介紹。只要遵循下面的基本規則即可：

"X, this is Y. Y, this is X."

「X，這是Y。Y，這是X。」

2.2a 介紹某人給另外一位認識 Introducing One Person to One Person

BIZ必通句型

❶ THIS IS..., THE...OF...

這位是……，……的……

例 This is Lydia Augustine, the Vice President of Sales.

這位是莉狄亞・奧古斯丁，業務部的副總裁。

例 This is Kim Carnes, the Director of our outreach program.
這位是金・卡恩斯，我們的推廣計畫總監。

❷ I WOULD LIKE TO INTRODUCE..., (THE...OF...).
我來介紹……
例 I would like to introduce Mark Schmeller, the chief researcher of our new project.
我來介紹一下，這位是馬克・史密勒，我們新專案的首席研究員。

❸ I WOULD LIKE YOU TO MEET..., (THE...OF...).
我為您介紹……
例 Mr. Smith, I would like you to meet Kenneth Johnson, the sales agent of Ironman Bikes.
史密斯先生，我為您介紹鐵人自行車的代理商肯尼士・強生。

❹ ALLOW ME TO INTRODUCE..., (THE...OF...).
容我介紹……
例 Allow me to introduce Bob Barker, our liaison.
容我來介紹鮑伯・巴克，我們的聯絡員。

❺ MAY I PRESENT..., (THE...OF...)?
我可以介紹……嗎？
例 May I present my friend, Jonathan?
我可以介紹我的朋友強納生嗎？

 Word list

liaison〔ˌlie`zɔ〕 *n.* 聯絡人

◇◇◇ 小心陷阱 ◇◇◇

☹ 錯誤用法
I would **like introduce** Becky.
我來介紹一下貝姬。

☺ 正確用法
I would **like to introduce** Becky.
我來介紹一下貝姬。

Show Time

❶ Mr. Tsai, I would like to introduce Rocky Marciano, our visitor from Pepsi Company in the U.S. Mr. Marciano, this is our company President, Mr. Tsai.

蔡先生，我來介紹一下，這位是從美國百事可樂公司來拜訪我們的洛基·馬西安諾。馬西安諾先生，這位是我們公司總裁蔡先生。

❷ Jacob, this is my colleague in the accounting division, Susan. Susan, this is Jacob, one of our customers from Poland.

雅各，這是我會計部的同事蘇珊。蘇珊，這位是雅各，我們的波蘭客戶之一。

2.2b 介紹某人給一群人認識
Introducing One Person to a Group of People

　　如果在一群人當中只有一位新面孔，那麼這群人就處於較高的地位。因此先介紹這位新面孔給這群人認識，然後再一一介紹每個人。

Show Time

Everybody, this is Mrs. Clayborn, the purchaser from Fine French Films in Paris. [Everybody says hi.] Mrs. Clayborn, allow me to introduce everyone.

各位，這位是巴黎傑出法國影片公司的克萊伯恩太太。〔大家打招呼〕克萊伯恩太太，容我介紹大家給妳認識。

接著，介紹者只需指向每個人，一個接著一個地介紹他們的名字，如果必要的話也說明職稱。介紹的時候通常是依據人們的地位順序一一進行：從高到低。

Show Time

This is our Vice President, Mr. Chang. This is our Marketing Director, Miss Lee. And this is our shop supervisor, Mr. Hu.

這位是我們的副總裁張先生。這位是我們的行銷主任李小姐。這位是我們的店長胡先生。

◇◇ 小心陷阱 ◇◇

☹ 錯誤用法
〔Introducing Joe〕**He** is our sales agent, Joe.
〔介紹喬〕他是我們的業務代理，喬。

☺ 正確用法
〔Introducing Joe〕**This** is our sales agent, Joe.
〔介紹喬〕這位是我們的業務代理，喬。

Word list

purchaser〔ˋpɝtʃəsɚ〕 *n.* 購買者

2.2c 當別人介紹你給某人的時候 When You are Introduced to Someone

當別人在介紹你的時候，讓介紹人完成介紹後才說「很高興認識您
(Nice to meet you.)」。以下說明正確的方法。

Show Time

> Harold : John, allow me to introduce Gretchen, our new
> customer from Finland. Gretchen, this is John,
> my colleague in the sales department.
> Gretchen : Nice to meet you.
> John : Nice to meet you, too.
>
> ----
>
> 哈諾 ：約翰，容我介紹葛瑞千，我們芬蘭的新客戶。葛瑞千，這
> 位是約翰，我業務部的同事。
> 葛瑞千：很高興認識你。
> 約翰 ：我也很高興認識你。

注意：約翰可以先說「很高興認識你」。誰先開口說這句話並沒有
關係。

上述的例子當中，葛瑞千和約翰都沒有重複他們的名字。這並沒有
必要，因為哈諾已經提到他們的名字兩次了！

2.3 交換名片 Exchanging Business Cards

當商務人士見面時，通常會互換名片。以下是這種情況使用的特定
用語。

ord list

Finland〔ˋfɪnlənd〕*n.* 芬蘭

2.3a 給對方你的名片 Offering Your Card

BIZ必通句型

❶ HERE IS MY (BUSINESS) CARD.
這是我的名片。

❷ LET ME GIVE YOU MY (BUSINESS) CARD.
讓我給您我的名片。

❸ I'D LIKE TO GIVE YOU MY (BUSINESS) CARD.
我要給您我的名片。

❹ MAY I GIVE YOU MY (BUSINESS) CARD?
我可以給您我的名片嗎？

❺ WOULD YOU LIKE MY (BUSINESS) CARD?
您要我的名片嗎？

2.3b 向對方要名片 Asking for a Card

BIZ必通句型

❶ DO YOU HAVE A BUSINESS CARD?
您有名片嗎？

❷ COULD YOU GIVE ME YOUR BUSINESS CARD?
能不能給我一張您的名片？

❸ MAY I HAVE YOUR BUSINESS CARD?
可以給我一張您的名片嗎?

◇◇◇ 小心陷阱 ◇◇◇

☹ 錯誤用法

Did you have a business card?

您有名片嗎?

☺ 正確用法

Do you have a business card?

您有名片嗎?

3 問候 Greeting People

「Greet」和「meet」不同。「Meet」可以指認識以往從未謀面的人,也可以指和朋友在某個特定地點見面,(各位還記得本章一開始的「BIZ 一點通」嗎?)「Greet」則表示打招呼。

◇◇◇ 小心陷阱 ◇◇◇

☹ 錯誤用法

Hi, Bob! Nice to **meet** you again.

嗨,鮑伯。很高興再見到你

☺ 正確用法

Hi, Bob! Nice to **see** you again.

嗨,鮑伯。很高興再見到你

3.1 稱謂 Terms of Address

稱謂的用語如下:

Mr.	用來稱呼所有的成年男性
Sir	可用來稱呼以往未曾謀面的男性
Mrs.	只能用來稱呼已婚女性
Ms.	用來稱呼女性(如果不知其已婚或未婚)
Miss	用來稱呼年輕的女性(不過有時候西方商場上的女性不接受這樣的稱呼)
Ma'am	用來稱呼以往未曾謀面的女性
職稱	只用在第一次的介紹時

★★★ *BIZ* 一點通 ★★★

「Miss」的音標和「Ms.」以及「Mrs.」的音標有著明顯的不同。在說這些稱謂時發音務必要清楚！

Miss〔mɪs〕
Ms.〔mɪz〕
Mrs.〔ˋmɪsɪz〕

Show Time

❶ This is the bank manager, Mr. Huang.
這位是銀行經理，黃先生。

❷ Excuse me, sir. Can you tell me where the restroom is?
對不起，先生，可否告訴我洗手間在哪裡？

❸ This is Mrs. Hu, our new supervisor.
這位是胡女士，我們新的主管。

❹ This is Ms. Forester. We just met in the elevator.
這位是佛若斯特女士。我們剛在電梯裡認識。

❺ Thanks for the coffee, Miss. The service at this restaurant is very good.
謝謝你的咖啡，小姐。這家餐廳的服務非常好。

❻ Pardon me, Ma'am. I was wondering if you could tell me which street the Hilton Hotel is on.
對不起，女士。不知您是否能夠告訴我希爾頓飯店在哪條街上？

❼ Welcome to our company! Let me introduce President Lin.
歡迎來我們公司！讓我介紹林總裁。

3.2 常見的問候和回應方式
Common Greetings and Responses

問候語包括你看到朋友、同事或熟人時所說的第一個字。

BIZ 必通句型

問候	回應
What's up? 怎麼樣啊？	**Nothing.** 沒什麼。 **Not much.** 沒什麼。
How are you? (How're you doing?) 你好嗎？	**Fine.** 好。 **Good.** 好。 **Great.** 很好。 **Wonderful.** 好極了。
How's it going? 怎麼樣啊？	**Fine.** 好。

	Good. 好。 Great. 很好。 Wonderful. 好極了。
Nice to see you. 很高興見到你。	Nice to see you, too. 我也很高興見到你。

★★★ *BIZ* 一點通 ★★★

說中文的人往往會以「吃飽了嗎？(Have you eaten yet?)」來問候彼此。這不過是表示「哈囉」的意思。你不能用同樣的方法來問候外國人。如果你跟外國人說「你吃飯了嗎？」他 / 她會以為你要邀請他們一塊吃飯。

◇◇◇ 小心陷阱 ◇◇◇

☹ 錯誤用法

A: What's up?

B: **Fine.**

A：怎麼樣啊？

B：好。

☺ 正確用法

A: What's up?

B: **Not much.**

A：怎麼樣啊？

B：沒什麼。

Remember the Principles

1 介紹別人及讓別人介紹自己都有公式可循。務必要了解這些公式。

There are formulas for giving and receiving introductions. Make sure you understand the formulas.

2 處理介紹的方法會讓人們對你的個性和特質留下深刻的印象。所以，務必要練習到能十分自然地運用介紹用語的地步。

The way you handle introductions will give people a strong impression of your personality and character. So, make sure you practice until you can handle the introduction language very naturally.

4 實戰演練 Partner Practice

依據下列情境，找個同伴一起模擬對話，作為實戰前的演練。

❶ A是台灣人。B是外國人，抵達台灣後在旅館或是飛機場等候。A
去旅館或是飛機場接B。

　　A：認出B

　　A：向B自我介紹

　　B：向A自我介紹

❷ A和B同在台北的商展上。

　　A：向B自我介紹

　　B：向A自我介紹

❸ A是台灣人。B是外國人，到A在台灣的公司拜訪。

　1) 想像你老闆在場

　　　A：向你的老闆介紹B

　2) 想像你的同事在場

　　　A：向一群你的同事介紹B

❹ A是台灣人，B是來台灣的外國人。你們在咖啡廳，假裝A的某位
同事走進咖啡廳。

　　A：向B介紹你的同事

第 **2** 章

談話
Conversation

　　我們在自我介紹之後，通常會開始談話。許多母語非英語的人開始和說英語的人談話時會感到緊張。這章將會介紹英語的對話過程以及指導各位如何展開、發展、以及總結談話的方法。用英語交談沒有你想像的那麼複雜。所以，準備好好享受和你有商務往來的西方人士的英文對話吧！

　　After we introduce ourselves to someone, we usually start a conversation. Many non-native English speakers feel nervous about starting a conversation with an English speaker. This chapter presents the English conversation process and teaches you how to begin, develop, and conclude a conversation. Having a conversation is not as complex as you might think. So, get prepared to enjoy English conversations with Westerners you have business contacts with!

1 談話的過程 The Conversation Process

談話是有過程的！如果你了解這樣的過程，你和西方人談話的時候會更自在。談話的過程包括四個部分：

1. 化解僵局
2. 聊天
3. 談話的進展
4. 談話的總結

在進一步解釋這四個部分之前，讓我們先看看談話過程中隨時都會發生的重要狀況：「忘了對方的姓名或是姓名的發音」。

BIZ必通句型

❶ I AM SORRY. I CAN'T RECALL YOUR NAME.
對不起，我忘了您的名字。

❷ COULD YOU TELL ME YOUR NAME AGAIN?
您可否再告訴我一次您的名字？

❸ MY MIND IS BLANK. I CAN'T RECALL YOUR NAME.
我的腦袋一片空白，我想不起您的名字。

❹ I AM SORRY. YOUR NAME ESCAPES ME.
對不起，我想不起您的名字。

❺ COULD YOU TELL ME HOW TO PRONOUNCE YOUR NAME AGAIN?
您可否再告訴我一次您的名字怎麼唸？

❻ COULD YOU PRONOUNCE YOUR NAME FOR ME AGAIN?

您可否再為我唸一次您的名字？

❼ I AM SORRY. I HAVE FORGOTTEN HOW TO PRONOUNCE YOUR NAME.

對不起，我已經忘了您名字怎麼唸。

◇◇◇ 小心陷阱 ◇◇◇

☹ 錯誤用法

Could you tell me how to **pronunciation** your name?

您可否告訴我您的名字要怎麼唸？

☺ 正確用法

Could you tell me how to **pronounce** your name?

您可否告訴我您的名字要怎麼唸？

2　化解僵局　Breaking the Ice

「化解僵局」的意思是和陌生人展開對話。這個步驟的重點在於：當兩個人頭一次見面時，會覺得緊張或是不知道要談些什麼，雙方之間有種冷冰冰的感覺——就好像冰塊一樣！雙方必須化解這樣的僵局，才能順利展開對話。

化解僵局的方法有以下這三種：

1. 以對方為話題的開端
2. 以某個情況為話題的開端
3. 以地點為話題的開端

這三種「破冰」的方法並沒有什麼特殊用語，各位只要發揮創意即可。以下做進一步的說明。

2.1 以對方為話題的開端　Commenting on the Individual

這是化解僵局最好的辦法。我們都喜歡受到別人的注意。所以，以對方為話題的開端可以拉近彼此的距離。只要張大眼睛，注意對方有什麼有趣的地方，然後以此作為話題的開端。只要不涉及個人的隱私，你可以針對衣著、珠寶、髮型等等發表你的看法。

Show Time

❶ That is a lovely dress.　Did you buy it here in Taipei?
這件洋裝好漂亮，你在台北買的嗎？

❷ That is an interesting watch.　Was it made in Japan?
這個手錶很有意思。這是日本製造的嗎？

❸ I see you have a folder from Canon camera company. Do you work for Canon?

我看到你有個佳能相機公司的資料夾，你是佳能的員工嗎？

◇◇ 小心陷阱 ◇◇

☹ 錯誤用法

Did you **bought** it in Taipei?

你在台北買的嗎？

☺ 正確用法

Did you **buy** it in Taipei?

你在台北買的嗎？

2.2 以某個情況為話題的開端 Commenting on the Situation

Show Time

❶ This is an interesting exhibition, don't you think?

這個展覽很有意思，你不覺得嗎？

❷ Do you attend these conferences often?

你常參加這些會議嗎？

❸ What do you think of the expo this year?

你覺得今年的博覽會如何？

Word list

folder〔`foldə〕n. 文書夾

exhibition〔ˌɛksəˈbɪʃən〕n. 展覽

expo〔`ɛkspo〕n.（萬國）博覽會（為 exposition 之略）

camera〔`kæmərə〕n. 照相機；攝影機

conference〔`kɑnfərəns〕n. 會議

❹ Is this your first time here? I don't think I have seen you before.

您是頭一次來這兒嗎？我想以前應該沒有見過您。

◇◇◇ 小心陷阱 ◇◇◇

☹ 錯誤用法

Did you attend these conferences often?

您經常參加這些會議嗎？

☺ 正確用法

Do you attend these conferences often?

您經常參加這些會議嗎？

2.3 以地點為話題的開端 Commenting on the Location

Show Time

❶ Have you been to Taipei before? This is an interesting city.

您以前來過台北嗎？這是個很有意思的城市。

❷ Is this your first time to Germany?

這是您第一次到德國嗎？

❸ This part of France is very pretty, don't you think?

法國的這部分地區非常漂亮，你不覺得嗎？

❹ This neighborhood is very nice—trees, flowers, and nice shops.

這附近很棒──有樹、有花、還有很棒的商店。

2.4 後續的問題 Follow-up Questions

許多打破僵局的問題都是「封閉式」的。所謂封閉式的問題就是可以「是」、或「不是」來回答的問句。在你問了這種封閉式的問題後，往往需要接著提出「開放性」的問題。開放性問題就不能光用「是」、或「不是」來回答。對方回答的時候往往需要提供些資訊或是表達自己的想法，因此有助於打開雙方的話題。

以下這個化解僵局的範例會讓各位了解如何運用開放性的問題：

Show Time

❶ 情境一：

對方說「Yes」之後的後續提問

A: That is an interesting watch. Is it made by a Japanese company?

B: Yes.

A: Can you tell me where you bought it? It might make a good gift for my son.

B: Sure, I bought it at the Seiko booth at Mitsukoshi. It's a little expensive, but it has many useful functions.

- -

A：這個手錶很有意思。這是日本廠商製造的嗎？

B：是的。

A：能告訴我你在哪裡買的嗎？這款手錶說不定很合適送給我兒子當禮物。

B：沒問題，我是在新光三越精工的專櫃買的。它有點貴，但具備很多實用的功能。

- -

對方說「No」之後的後續提問

A: That is an interesting watch. Is it made by a Japanese

company?

B: No.

A: Where is it made? I thought only Japanese companies made such watches.

B: It's made in Switzerland. The Swiss make fine watches, too.

A：這個手錶很有意思。這是日本廠商製造的嗎？

B：不是。

A：那是哪裡製造的？我以為只有日本公司會作這種手錶。

B：這是瑞士製造的。瑞士人也製造很棒的手錶。

❷ 情境二：

對方說「No」之後的後續提問

A: Is this your first time to Germany?

B: No. I have been here many times.

A: Oh. What do you think of the German people? I don't know much about their culture.

B: Well, the Germans are hard-working and serious. They can also be friendly. They are mainly praised for their incredible efficiency.

A：這是你第一次到德國嗎？

B：不是，我已經來過好幾次。

Word list

Switzerland〔`swɪtsələnd〕*n.* 瑞士　　　Swiss〔swɪs〕*n.* 瑞士人

praise〔prez〕*v.* 稱讚

incredible〔ɪn`krɛdəbḷ〕*adj.* 驚人的；非常的

A：喔，你覺得德國人怎麼樣？我不是很清楚他們的文化。

B：嗯，德國人工作很勤奮，而且很嚴肅。他們也能很友善，他們驚人的效率最為世人稱讚。

對方說「Yes」之後的後續提問

A: Is this your first time to Germany?

B: Yes.

A: Mine, too. What do you think of the country so far?

B: Well, the country is pretty. I like the old buildings a lot.

A：這是您第一次到德國嗎？

B：是的。

A：我也是第一次。到目前為止，你覺得這個國家怎麼樣？

B：嗯，這個國家很漂亮。我非常喜歡那些古老的建築。

3 聊天 Small Talk

「聊天」是針對一些無關痛癢的話題進行對話。聊天的目的是在進入真正重要的主題（如：談生意）之前，先聊些輕鬆的話題。你可以透過聊天更深入了解對方，藉以建立雙方的關係。

3.1 好的話題 Good Topics

以下都是一些適合聊天的話題。當你開始聊天的時候，記得有時候可能需要利用後續的問題來延續雙方的對話。

Weather 天氣	Hobbies 嗜好	Travel 旅遊
Sports 運動	Books 書籍	Music 音樂
Current Events 當前大事	Family 家庭	Movies 電影
Food 食物		

★★★ BIZ 一點通 ★★★

西方人聊天的時候經常以天氣作為話題。所以，如果你碰到個西方人，準備談談天氣吧！

3.1a 聊天的開場白 Opening Topics for Small Talk

以下提供一些範例，說明如何以上述的各種話題打開話匣子。聊天的開場白其實並沒有什麼特殊的用語。只要問你覺得有意思、而且對方也願意回答的問題即可。

Show Time

❶ WEATHER

天氣

例 The weather is really hot. Is it always like this here?

天氣實在很熱。這裡是不是都這麼熱？

❷ HOBBIES

嗜好

例 What do you like to do in your spare time?

你空閒的時候喜歡作些什麼？

◇◇◇ 小心陷阱 ◇◇◇

☹ 錯誤用法

What you like to do in your spare time?

你空閒的時候喜歡作些什麼？

☺ 正確用法

What **do** you like to do in your spare time?

你空閒的時候喜歡作些什麼？

❸ TRAVEL

旅遊

例 Do you travel to Asian countries on business often?

你經常到亞洲國家出差嗎？

❹ SPORTS

運動

例 I read in the paper that San Antonio's basketball team is doing very well this year. Do you watch professional basketball games?

我看到報上說聖安東尼奧的籃球隊今年的表現非常好。你看不看職業籃球賽？

⑤ BOOKS
書籍

例 I am reading a very good book about using principles of war in business. Have you read any interesting books lately?

我正在讀一本有關在商場上運用作戰原則的好書。你最近有沒有讀到什麼有趣的書？

⑥ MUSIC
音樂

例 What kind of music do you like to listen to?

你喜歡聽什麼樣的音樂？

⑦ CURRENT EVENTS
當前的大事

例 OPEC's annual meeting is beginning tomorrow. Do you know if anything important will be decided there?

石油輸出國家組織的年度會議將於明天開始。你知道屆時會作出什麼重要的決定嗎？

Word list

OPEC〔ˋopɛk〕 *n.* 石油輸出國家組織（Organization of Petroleum Exporting Countries 的縮寫）

◇◇◇ 小心陷阱 ◇◇◇

☹ 錯誤用法

Do you know anything important will be decided there?

你知道屆時會作出什麼重要的決定嗎？

☺ 正確用法

Do you know **if** anything important will be decided there?

你知道屆時會作出什麼重要的決定嗎？

---

⑧ FAMILY

家庭

例 Do you have any photos of your family?

你有沒有任何家人的照片？

---

⑨ MOVIES

電影

例 The new *Star Wars* movie opens this weekend. Are you going to see it?

新的星際大戰電影將在這個週末開始上映。你會去看嗎？

---

⑩ FOOD

食物

例 Is it difficult to get used to the spicy food here?

適應這裡口味很辣的食物是否很難？

Word list

open〔`opən〕v.（電影）開始上映

3.1b 重要的建議　Important Advice

　　1. 注意當前的大事：西方的商務人士會透過閱讀報紙、雜誌、以及網路上的資訊，時時掌握當前發生的大事。西方人在聊天的時候常常會以這些當前大事作為話題。對於西方人而言，不論是什麼性質的談話（就算只是聊天而已），資訊交流都是個重要的環節。當前大事提供一些西方人喜歡在談話中運用的資訊。閱讀英文報紙是掌握當前大事的好辦法（而且有助提升你的英文能力，特別是字彙！）

　　2. 不要問對方會覺得尷尬的問題：許多台灣人會問外國人以下這些問題：

"Do you like Taiwan?"

「你喜歡台灣嗎？」

"Do you like Chinese food?"

「你喜歡中國菜嗎？」

　　這些都不算是好的問題。對方可能不喜歡台灣或是中國菜。如果這個人回答「不」，那你會覺得不開心。如果對方回答「是」，那他／她會因為對你說謊而感到不舒服。

　　運用開放性的問題，可以獲得正面的回答，而且避免尷尬的情況。以下是一些範例：

Show Time

❶ What kind of Chinese food do you like?
你喜歡哪一種中國菜？

❷ What is your favorite Chinese food?
你最喜歡的中國菜是哪一道？

❸ What is the most interesting thing you have seen in Taiwan?
你在台灣看到最有意思的東西是什麼？

☹ 錯誤用法

What is the most interesting thing you **had saw** in Taiwan?

你在台灣看到最有意思的東西是什麼？

☺ 正確用法

What is the most interesting thing you **have seen** in Taiwan?

你在台灣看到最有意思的東西是什麼？

❹ What would you like to see in Taiwan?
你想在台灣看到什麼？

❺ What is surprising to you about Taiwan?
台灣什麼地方會讓你覺得驚訝？

3. 你可以準備聊天的題材：譬如，如果你將和某位外國人見面，你可以事先挑個聊天的話題，並準備幾個可以開啟對話的開放性問題。

3.2 危險的話題 Dangerous Topics

以下是危險的聊天話題。這些話題並不是絕對不好，比如，有些人很開放，不論是什麼話題都樂於討論！有些人很隨和，不管你說什麼都不會生氣。不過建議各位最好還是遵循以下這個原則：

1. 和陌生人聊天時千萬不要挑以下這些話題。

2. 當你和熟人（熟悉對方的個性、人格、生活的某些細節）聊天時，如果你非常確定對方對這些話題有興趣，而且不會覺得不舒服，那你可以從以下話題挑選一個進行討論。

Controversial topics:	Personal matters:	Bad news:
abortion, politics, religion	age, weight, health, sex, salary	recent crimes, recent disasters
具有爭議性的話題：	個人的私事：	壞消息：
墮胎、政治、宗教	年紀、體重、健康、性、薪水	最近發生的犯罪、災害

Word list

controversial〔͵kɑntrə`vɝʃəl〕*adj.* 引起爭論的
abortion〔ə`bɔrʃən〕*n.* 墮胎；流產　　disaster〔dɪz`æstə〕*n.* 災害

4 談話的進展 Developing Conversations

4.1 專注在對方身上 Focusing on the Other Person

發展談話的關鍵在以對方的興趣為焦點。發問是找出對方興趣的方法。一直問到你找到談話的好題材為止。然後，談談這個話題。接著利用其他問題引導對方談談他／她的感受、態度、想法、信念。可以使用下列問題：

BIZ必通句型

❶ HOW DO YOU FEEL ABOUT...?
你覺得……怎麼樣？

❷ WHAT DO YOU THINK ABOUT...?
你對……有什麼看法？

❸ WHAT IS YOUR OPINION?
你的意見如何？

❹ WHAT ARE YOUR THOUGHTS ABOUT THAT?
你對那有何想法？

❺ WHAT IS YOUR POINT OF VIEW?
你的觀點如何？

◇◇◇ 小心陷阱 ◇◇◇

☹ 錯誤用法

How do you think about that?

你對那有何想法？

☺ 正確用法

What do you think about that?

你對那有何想法？

4.2 尋求了解 Seeking Understanding

如果你不了解對方所說的話，應該發問加以釐清。對方也希望你能理解他的話，所以若你提出問題釐清自己不了解、或是不確定的地方，他會很樂意回答。

4.2a 釐清語言的方法 Language-related Comments

有時候不了解對方可能是因為語言的障礙。如果出現這樣的狀況，可以問下列這些問題讓對方知道你希望更清楚地了解他。

BIZ必通句型

★關於「意思」或「發音」方面的釐清方法

❶ **COULD/WOULD YOU REPEAT THAT, PLEASE?**
能 / 可否請您重複一遍？

❷ **COULD/WOULD YOU SAY THAT AGAIN, PLEASE?**
能 / 可否請您再說一遍？

❸ COULD/WOULD YOU SAY THAT AGAIN USING SIMPLE LANGUAGE?

您能 / 可否用簡單的說法再說一遍？

❹ COULD/WOULD YOU WRITE THAT DOWN?

您能 / 可否把它寫下來？

◇◇◇ 小心陷阱 ◇◇◇

☹ 錯誤用法

Could you **write down that**?

您可否把它寫下來？

☺ 正確用法

Could you **write that down**?

您可否把它寫下來？

BIZ必通句型

★對方說得太快時的釐清方法

❶ COULD/WOULD YOU SPEAK A LITTLE MORE SLOWLY, PLEASE?

能 / 可否請您說慢一點？

❷ COULD/WOULD YOU SPEAK A LITTLE SLOWER, PLEASE?

能 / 可否請您說慢一點？

❸ COULD/WOULD YOU REPEAT THAT SLOWLY?

你能 / 可否放慢速度重複一遍？

❹ COULD/WOULD YOU SAY THAT AGAIN SLOWLY?
您能／可否放慢速度再說一次？

> ★★★ *BIZ*一點通 ★★★
> 「could」和「would」這兩個字的差別僅在於「could」的語氣比較委婉，或許也可以說比較禮貌。不過只是些微的差別而已！

4.2b 釐清對方意思的方法　Clarifying

　　即使在和說同種語言的人溝通時，有時候仍需對所說的話加以釐清。問題不在於你說的或是聽的語言是外國話，而是因為人沒有完美的，有時候是說話者說話的方法令人困惑，有時候是聽話者跟不上對方思考的速度。所以，不管是以哪種語言談話，釐清意思在對談時都是很正常的。以下利用幾個範例說明常見的釐清方法。

BIZ必通句型

❶ YOU ARE SAYING..., RIGHT?
你是說……，對嗎？
例 You are saying the traffic is bad at 5:00, right?
你是說五點鐘的交通很糟糕，對嗎？

❷ YOU MEAN..., RIGHT?
你的意思是……，對嗎？
例 You mean the plane will be delayed one hour, right?
你的意思是說這班飛機會延誤一個小時，對嗎？

❸ YOU ARE SAYING... IS THAT RIGHT?
你是說……，對不對？

例 You are saying the expenditure amount is not enough. Is that right?

你是說這筆經費的金額不夠，對不對？

❹ **YOU MEAN... IS THAT RIGHT?**

你的意思是……，對不對？

例 You mean we cannot leave until the meeting is finished. Is that right?

你的意思是我們得等到會議結束才能離開，對不對？

❺ **DO YOU MEAN...?**

你的意思是……？

例 Do you mean that the designs won't be finished until March?

你的意思是說要到三月份這個設計才能完成嗎？

◇◇◇ 小心陷阱 ◇◇◇

☹ 錯誤用法

Your meaning he is wrong?

你是說他錯了？

☺ 正確用法

You mean he is wrong?

你是說他錯了？

5 談話的總結　Concluding Conversations

　　談話的結束可以簡單、也可能很困難，要看情況而定。如果談話告一段落，而且雙方都準備離開，那麼結束就很容易。如果談話還沒告一段落，但你卻得離開對方（不管是什麼理由），你可能會對結束這段對話感到不自在，也可能會覺得這麼做很沒有禮貌。但對於西方人而言，這絕對不是沒有禮貌的事情。

5.1 結束尚未告一段落的談話
Ending an Unfinished Conversation

　　西方人一般來說都是以時間為中心的（除了法國、義大利、以及西班牙）。他們非常重視時間，日常生活亦較規律。結果就是西方人往往會突然地結束談話，因為他們得趕去作某些別的事情。西方人對此相當習慣，如果談話當中某人得離開，他們也不會因此覺得不高興。

　　如果你希望盡量有禮貌，只要讓對方知道你為什麼必須離開，以及其實你還很想繼續談下去就可以了。以下例句是結束談話的常見方法。

*BIZ*必通句型

❶ I'M SORRY, BUT I HAVE TO LEAVE.
對不起，我得離開了。

❷ I'M SORRY, BUT I HAVE TO GO.
對不起，我得走了。

❸ I'M SORRY, BUT I HAVE TO RUN.
對不起，我得趕緊離開了。

以下說明如何表達其實你還希望繼續談話的方法。

BIZ必通句型

❶ LET'S TALK AGAIN LATER!
讓我們稍後再談！

❷ I HOPE WE CAN TALK MORE LATER!
我希望我們稍後可以再多談些！

❸ I LOOK FORWARD TO TALKING TO YOU AGAIN NEXT TIME!
我期待和你下次再談！

❹ WE'LL TALK MORE LATER, OKAY?
我們稍後再談，好嗎？

❺ WE'LL TALK MORE NEXT TIME, OKAY?
我們下次再談，好嗎？

❻ WE'LL PICK THIS UP LATER!
我們稍後再繼續談這個話題！

Word list

look forward to〔lʊk ˋfɔrwəd tu〕v. 期待

◇◇◇ 小心陷阱 ◇◇◇

☹ 錯誤用法

I **wish** we can talk more later.

我希望我們稍後可以繼續再談。

☺ 正確用法

I **hope** we can talk more later.

我希望我們稍後可以繼續再談。

Show Time

❶ I am sorry, but I have to go. I have an appointment. Let's talk again later!

對不起，我得走了。我有個約會，我們稍後再談！

❷ I am sorry, but I have to leave. My husband is here to pick me up. I hope we can talk more later!

對不起，我得離開了。我先生來這兒接我。希望我們稍後可以再多談些！

❸ I am sorry, but I have to run. I need to get back to the office. I look forward to talking to you again next time!

對不起，我得趕緊離開了。我得趕回辦公室。期待下回和你再談！

❹ I am sorry, but I have to go. I am late for a meeting. We'll talk more next time, okay?

對不起，我得走了。我開會遲到了。我們下回再多談些，好嗎？

5.2 結束業已告一段落的談話
Ending a Completed Conversation

當談話已經告一段落，禮貌上應該說些客套話。

BIZ 必通句型

❶ IT WAS NICE TALKING WITH YOU.
和您談話很高興。

❷ I ENJOYED TALKING WITH YOU.
我很高興和您談話。

❸ IT WAS FUN TO TALK WITH YOU.
和您談話很有趣。

❹ IT WAS INTERESTING TO TALK WITH YOU.
和您談話很有意思。

❺ THAT WAS A NICE CONVERSATION.
我們談得很愉快。

❻ I LOOK FORWARD TO OUR NEXT CONVERSATION.
我期待我們下次的談話。

◇◇◇ 小心陷阱 ◇◇◇

☹ 錯誤用法
I enjoyed **talk** with you.
很高興和您談話。

☺ 正確用法
I enjoyed **talking** with you.
很高興和您談話。

Remember the Principles

1 問問題對於建立良好的對話是很重要的。有效運用問題,並且鼓勵人們多談談自己,可以形成愉快的對話以及建立彼此之間的關係。此外,如果開口說英文讓你覺得緊張,可以利用問題讓對方盡可能地多講!

Questions are very important for building good conversations. Use questions effectively, and encourage people to talk about themselves. This will produce a pleasant conversation and also build the interpersonal relationship. In addition, if you feel nervous about speaking English, you can use questions to keep the other person talking as much as possible!

Word list

interpersonal〔͵ɪntɚˋpɝsn̩l〕 *adj.* 人際關係的

2 好好享受你們的談話！不要把心思專注在自己的發音、字彙、和文法上。應該把重心放在關係的培養上。你愈是為對方和你的關係著想，就會覺得愈自在，而且你們的談話也會更加地成功。

Enjoy your conversations! Don't focus your thoughts on your pronunciation, vocabulary, and grammar. Focus on developing a relationship. The more you think about the other person and the relationship, the more relaxed you will feel and the more successful your conversation will be.

6 實戰演練　Partner Practice

依據下列情境，找個同伴一起模擬對話，作為實戰前的演練。

1 A 和 B 都在台北的貿易商展上。他們並不認識彼此。 A 想開口和 B 談話。

1) A：開口評論一下B，藉以化解僵局。

B：聊聊天氣，藉以開口談話。

A & B：開始談話。利用問句，把重心放在彼此身上。

2) A：以情境為話題化解僵局。

B：聊聊目前的大事，藉以開始談話。

A & B：開始談話。利用問句，把重心放在彼此身上。

3) A：以地點為話題化解僵局。

B：聊聊當地的食物，藉以開始談話。

A & B：開始談話。利用問句，把重心放在彼此身上。

2 重複以上的1)、2) 和3)，但地點是洛杉磯的貿易商展上。

第 **3** 章

交際和接待
Socializing & Entertainment

　　和國際訪客做生意的重要環節之一，便是交際和接待客人。交際和接待可以在談生意之前、之後，甚至在談生意的時候進行。這一章提供的用語，將讓各位和外國訪客有個愉快的體驗。

　　An important part of doing business with international visitors is socializing and entertaining.　Socializing and entertaining can come before, after, and even during business.　This chapter provides the English that will allow you to have enjoyable experiences with your foreign visitors.

1 基本的資訊　Basic Information

1.1 基本字彙　Basic Vocabulary

BIZ必通字彙

人物 (People)
❶ host〔host〕 *n.* 主人　　　❷ guest〔gɛst〕 *n.* 客人
❸ colleague〔`kɑlig〕 *n.* 同事
❹ acquaintance〔ə`kwentəns〕 *n.* 熟人

有關錢的事情 (Money Matters)
❶ bill〔bɪl〕 *n.* 帳單
❷ cashier〔kæ`ʃɪr〕 *n.* 櫃檯收帳員
❸ receipt〔rɪ`sit〕 *n.* 收據　　❹ expense〔ɪk`spɛns〕 *n.* 費用

Show Time

❶ I will be your **host** tonight. Let's go out and have a nice time.
今晚我當主人，我們出去享受一下。

❷ In Taiwan you are my **guest**. Let me try to show you a good time in Taiwan.
在台灣你是我的客人。讓我帶你在台灣好好地玩一下。

❸ My **colleague** will join us for lunch.
我同事將會和我們共進午餐。

④ I see an **acquaintance** of mine at that table.
我看到那桌有個我認識的人。

⑤ Let me pay the **bill**.
讓我來付帳。

⑥ We can ask the **cashier** for change.
我們可以跟櫃檯換零錢。

⑦ Can I get a **receipt** for this?
可不可以給我一張收據？

⑧ I need to keep track of all my **expenses**.
我需要掌握我所有的花費。

1.2 最重要的規則 Most Important Rule

最重要的原則是設身處地為訪客著想。將客人的需求和渴望置於自己的需求之上。記得，人們在外國時，有些需求和渴望是本地人看不到的。所以，你得仔細觀察，並且盡可能地協助你的客人。你的訪客會因你的殷勤接待而感到開心。

2 不同的場合　Places to Go

　　記住上個部分提到的重要原則。不同的人喜歡的事物各有不同，所以，試著去發現你的訪客可能喜歡哪類型的娛樂。有些人喜歡去海邊，有些人則喜歡到山上；有些人喜歡去咖啡館，有些人則喜歡上酒館；有些人喜歡博物館或是古老建築之類有歷史意義的地方，有些人則喜歡唱歌、跳舞之類的大眾化娛樂。

　　不管去哪裡——餐廳、酒館、你家、任何地方——你都需要提供飲食。而當別人提供你飲食時，你也須恰當地回應。以下將提供在這些情況中所需的用語。

2.1 提供飲食　Offering Food and Drink

BIZ必通句型

❶ WOULD YOU LIKE...?
你想要……嗎？
例 Would you like a glass of water?
　要不要來杯水？
例 Would you like some peanuts?
　要不要來點花生？

❷ CAN I GET YOU...?
我可以拿些……給你嗎？
例 Can I get you a beer?
　要不要我幫你拿瓶啤酒？
例 Can I get you some soup?
　要不要我幫你拿點湯？

❸ HOW ABOUT...?

……如何？

例 How about a Coke?

來瓶可樂如何？

例 How about some fresh fruit?

來些新鮮的水果如何？

❹ WHAT ABOUT...?

……怎麼樣？

例 What about an apple?

來顆蘋果怎麼樣？

例 What about some fried vegetables?

來些炸蔬菜怎麼樣？

❺ WOULD YOU CARE FOR...?

你想要……嗎？

例 Would you care for a glass of wine?

想不想來杯酒？

例 Would you care for ice cream?

想不想來點冰淇淋？

◇◇◇ 小心陷阱 ◇◇◇

☹ 錯誤用法

Can I **got** you some tea?

要不要我幫你弄些茶？

☺ 正確用法

Can I **get** you some tea?

要不要我幫你弄些茶？

Show Time

★「How about...?」以及「What about...?」這兩種問句只能用在提供選擇的情況。

❶ We can have apple juice or orange juice. How about apple juice?
我們可以喝蘋果汁或柳橙汁。蘋果汁如何？

❷ There are many places where we can eat. How about Cantonese food?
我們可以用餐的地方很多。廣東菜如何？

❸ We can go to a park or a museum or a theater. Oh, I know! What about a hot spring?
我們可以去公園、博物館、或戲院。喔，我知道了！去泡個溫泉怎麼樣？

❹ How about going to the harbor to look at the ships?
去海港看船如何？

2.2 回應的方法　Responding to Offers

BIZ必通句型

❶ I WOULD LOVE...
我想要……

Word list

Cantonese〔͵kæntən`iz〕 *adj.* 廣東的　　hot spring〔`hɑt `sprɪŋ〕 *n.* 溫泉

例 I would love some wine. Thanks.
我想來些酒，謝謝。

例 I would love some fresh fruit.
我想來些新鮮的水果。

❷ THAT WOULD BE NICE.
那很好。

❸ A/SOME...WOULD BE NICE.
來個／來些……會很好。

例 A Coke would be nice. Thanks.
來瓶可樂很好，謝謝。

例 Some nuts would be nice. Thanks.
來些花生很好，謝謝。

❹ THAT WOULD BE GREAT.
那很棒。

❺ A/SOME...WOULD BE GREAT.

例 A cup of coffee would be great.
來杯咖啡很棒。

例 Some popcorn would be great. Thanks.
來些爆米花很棒，謝謝。

❻ SURE.
當然。

❼ I DON'T... BUT THANKS FOR ASKING.
我不……不過謝謝你問我。

例 I don't drink alcohol. But thanks for asking.
我不喝酒，不過謝謝你問我。

例 I don't eat beef. But thanks for asking.
我不吃牛肉，不過謝謝你問我。

❽ I SHOULDN'T... BUT THANKS FOR ASKING.
我不應該⋯⋯不過謝謝你問我。

例 I shouldn't eat so soon after breakfast. But thanks for asking.
早餐後我不應該這麼快就吃東西。不過謝謝你問我。

例 I shouldn't drink things with caffeine because of my health. But thanks for asking.
因為健康問題，我不應該喝任何含咖啡因的東西。不過謝謝你問我。

❾ NO, THANK YOU.
不了，謝謝。

◇◇◇ 小心陷阱 ◇◇◇

☹ 錯誤用法
I don't like pork, but thanks **for your asking**.
我不喜歡豬肉，不過謝謝你問我。

☺ 正確用法
I don't like pork, but thanks **for asking**.
我不喜歡豬肉，不過謝謝你問我。

Word list

caffeine〔`kæfiɪn〕*n.* 咖啡因

Show Time

❶ Host : Can I get you a cup of Chinese red tea?
Guest : A cup of tea would be nice.
Host : Alright, let me go make some. I'll be right back.

主人：要不要我幫你弄杯中式紅茶？
客人：來杯茶很好。
主人：好，我去泡，馬上回來。

❷ Host : Would you care for a banana?
Guest : I can't eat one now. I am still full from that great
         lunch. But thanks for asking. Maybe later.
Host : No problem.

主人：要不要來根香蕉？
客人：我現在吃不下。用了那頓豐盛的午餐，我現在還很飽。不過謝
     謝你問我。可能待會吧。
主人：沒問題。

3 邀請 Inviting

3.1 正式的邀請 Formal Invitations

　　主人需對訪客提出特定的邀請，不應該光是問「你今晚想要做什麼？」。理由有二，第一，訪客人在陌生的國度，可能不知道有哪些娛樂；第二，主人主動提出邀請是很合乎禮節的。這顯示主人會為客人著想，而且試圖讓客人開心。

3.1a 提出邀請 Making an Invitation

> **BIZ必通句型**

❶ I WOULD LIKE TO INVITE YOU FOR...
　我想要邀請你……
　例 I would like to invite you for lunch this afternoon.
　　我想邀你今日下午共進午餐。
　例 I would like to invite you for dinner on Tuesday evening.
　　我想邀你週二晚上共進晚餐。

❷ I WOULD LIKE TO INVITE YOU TO...
　我想要邀請你去……
　例 I would like to invite you to a traditional performance this
　　weekend.
　　我想邀你觀賞本週末的一項傳統表演。
　例 I would like to invite you to a dance party.
　　我想邀請你參加舞會。

❸ I WAS WONDERING IF YOU WOULD LIKE TO...

我在想你要不要⋯⋯

例 I was wondering if you would like to visit a museum with me tomorrow.

我在想你明天要不要和我去參觀博物館。

例 I was wondering if you would like to have breakfast with me tomorrow morning.

我在想你明天早上要不要和我共進早餐。

❹ WOULD YOU BE INTERESTED IN...?

你有沒有興趣⋯⋯？

例 Would you be interested in attending a business lunch with me?

你會不會有興趣和我共進商業午餐？

例 Would you be interested in going to a concert?

你會不會有興趣去聽演唱會？

❺ WOULD YOU LIKE TO...?

你想要⋯⋯嗎？

例 Would you like to go to a party with us tonight?

你今晚想和我們去參加一個派對嗎？

例 Would you like to take a drive to the coast tomorrow afternoon?

你明天下午想坐車到海邊兜風嗎？

❻ ARE YOU FREE FOR/TO...?

你有沒有空⋯⋯？

例 Are you free for supper Friday night?

星期五晚上你有沒有空共進晚餐？

例 Are you free to see a movie after our meeting?
我們的會議結束後，你有沒有空去看個電影？

❼ SHALL WE...?
我們……吧？
例 Shall we have breakfast together?
我們一起吃早餐吧？

◇◇◇ 小心陷阱 ◇◇◇

☹ 錯誤用法
Would you be **interesting** in some fresh fruit?
你有沒有興趣來些新鮮的水果？
☺ 正確用法
Would you be **interested** in some fresh fruit?
你有沒有興趣來些新鮮的水果？

3.1b 回應他人的邀請 Responding to an Invitation

*BIZ*必通句型

❶ THAT SOUNDS GREAT.
那聽起來很棒。

❷ SOUNDS GOOD.
聽起來不錯。

❸ LET'S GO!
我們走吧！

❹ WHY NOT?!

為什麼不?!

❺ THAT'S A GREAT IDEA!

那是個很棒的點子!

❻ I'M AFRAID I...

恐怕我……

例 I'm afraid I can't attend tonight.

恐怕我今晚不能參加。

例 I'm afraid I don't have time to join you tomorrow.

恐怕我明天沒有時間加入你們的行列。

❼ I WISH I COULD, BUT...

但願我可以,可是……

例 I wish I could, but I already have an appointment for this afternoon.

但願我可以,但是我今天下午已經安排了約會。

例 I wish I could, but I am really tired and better get some rest.

但願我可以,不過我真得很累,最好休息一下。

❽ THANKS FOR THE INVITATION, BUT...

謝謝你的邀請,不過……

例 Thanks for the invitation, but I have to see the doctor tomorrow morning.

謝謝你的邀請,不過我明天得去看醫生。

例 Thanks for the invitation, but my meeting will last all day.

謝謝你的邀請,不過我要開一整天的會。

❾ I'D LOVE TO, BUT...

我很樂意，不過……

例 I'd love to, but the boss already invited me to dinner.

我很樂意，不過老闆已先邀我去吃晚飯。

例 I'd love to, but I don't have the energy to climb the mountain.

我很樂意，不過我沒有力氣爬山。

◇◇◇ 小心陷阱 ◇◇◇

☹ 錯誤用法

Thanks for your **inviting**, but I can't go tonight.

謝謝你的邀請，不過我今晚不能去。

☺ 正確用法

Thanks for your **invitation**, but I can't go tonight.

謝謝你的邀請，不過我今晚不能去。

Show Time

❶ Host : Would you like to see a traditional Chinese lion dance downtown tonight?

Guest : That sounds great. What time will we leave?

Host : Six o'clock.

主人：你今晚想不想去市中心看傳統的中國舞獅？

客人：聽起來很棒。我們幾點鐘出發？

主人：六點鐘。

❷ Host : Would you like to have dinner at a new Italian restaurant tonight?

Guest : I'd love to, but I have to attend an emergency

> meeting tonight.
> Host : That's alright. Maybe tomorrow.
>
> ---
>
> 主人：你今晚想不想到一家新開的義大利餐廳吃晚餐？
> 客人：我很樂意，不過我今晚得參加一場緊急會議。
> 主人：沒關係，或許明天吧。

3.2 其他的選擇 Alternatives

提出邀請最好的方法就是提供選擇。如果不知道你的訪客喜歡哪種食物，那就提供兩個或是兩個以上的地方讓對方選擇。敏感、而且明智的主人會適時地提供客人選擇的機會。

3.2a 提供其他選擇的方法 Offering Alternatives

BIZ必通句型

❶ WOULD YOU RATHER...OR...?
你想要……或……？
例 Would you rather go to an Italian restaurant or a Chinese restaurant?
你想去義大利餐廳，還是中國餐廳？
例 Would you rather eat fish or chicken?
你想吃魚，還是雞？

❷ WOULD YOU PREFER...OR...?
你比較想要……還是……？
例 Would you prefer to see a movie or visit a park?
你比較想看電影，還是去參觀公園？

例 Would you prefer visiting the zoo or seeing the outdoor concert?

你比較想要參觀動物園,還是去看露天演唱會?

例 Would you prefer juice or coffee?

你比較想喝果汁,還是咖啡?

❸ **WHICH SOUNDS BETTER, ...OR...?**

哪個聽起來比較好,……或……?

例 Which sounds better, going to the beach or playing golf?

哪個聽起來比較好,去海邊還是去打高爾夫球?

例 Which sounds better, a night market or a nice restaurant?

哪個聽起來比較好,去夜市還是去家好餐廳?

❹ **WOULD...OR...BE BETTER FOR YOU?**

對你來說,……還是……比較好?

例 Would beef or pork be better for you?

對你來說,牛肉還是豬肉比較好?

例 Would the art museum or KTV be better for you?

對你來說,美術館還是 KTV 比較好?

❺ **WE COULD..., OR WE COULD...**

我們可以……,或者我們可以……

例 We could go shopping, or we could watch the Dragon Boat races.

我們可以去購物,或者我們可以去看龍舟賽。

例 We could have some Taiwanese ice cream, or we could buy some fresh nuts.

我們可以來些台灣冰淇淋,或是我們可以買些新鮮的堅果。

∘∘◇ 小心陷阱 ◇∘∘

☹ 錯誤用法

Would you rather **swimming** or **hiking**?

你想要游泳還是健行？

☺ 正確用法

Would you rather **swim** or **hike**?

你想游泳還是健行？

3.2b 對於其他選擇的回應技巧 Responding to Alternatives

BIZ必通句型

❶ I WOULD RATHER...

我寧可……

例 I would rather go to the gym.

我寧可去健身房。

❷ I PREFER...

我偏好……

例 I prefer action movies.

我偏好動作片。

❸ ...SOUNDS GOOD.

……聽起來不錯。

例 Going to the mountain sounds good.

上山去聽起來不錯。

❹ ...SOUNDS BETTER.

……聽起來比較好。

例 Visiting the science museum sounds better.
參觀科學館聽起來比較好。

⑤ I'LL GO FOR...
我選擇……
例 I'll go for the trip to the beach.
我選擇到海邊去。

◇◇◇ 小心陷阱 ◇◇◇

☹ 錯誤用法
I would rather **walking**.
我寧可走路。

☺ 正確用法
I would rather **walk**.
我寧可走路。

Show Time

❶ Host : Would you prefer shopping at Sogo or having a cup of coffee at Starbucks?
Guest : I would rather go to Starbucks.
Host : Alright. There is one nearby. Let's go!

主人：你比較想去 Sogo 購物還是去星巴克喝杯咖啡？
客人：我寧可去星巴克。
主人：好，附近就有一家。我們走吧！

❷ Host : We could take a walk in the park, or we could take a look at one of the traditional streets downtown.
Guest : Visiting a traditional street sounds good.

Host ：Okay. Let's drive there in my car.

主人：我們可以去公園散步，或者可以去市中心的傳統街道之一看看。

客人：參觀傳統街道聽起來很有意思。

主人：好，開我的車過去吧。

4 出外吃飯 Eating Out

　　不同的國家各有不同的食物，這點大家都知道。沒有人會喜歡外國所有的食物。事實上，就算是自己國家的食物，也沒有人會全部都喜歡！所以，了解你的訪客，並且試著找出他偏好的口味。鹹的？甜的？辣的？牛肉？雞肉？等等。如果對訪客國家的食物沒有概念，而且實在猜不出客人可能會喜歡什麼食物，乾脆直接問他吧！

4.1 提議請客 Offering to Pay

BIZ必通句型

❶ IT'S ON ME.
我請客。
例 Oh, you don't need to pay. It's on me.
喔，你不用付帳，我請客。

❷ IT'S MY TREAT.
我請客。
例 I'm glad you enjoyed the food. It's my treat.
我很高興你喜歡這菜色，我請客。

❸ I GOT IT.
我拿到了。
例 Here comes the waiter with the bill. I got it.
服務生拿帳單來了，我拿到了。

❹ I'LL TAKE CARE OF THE BILL.
我來付帳。

例 You don't need your money this time. I'll take care of the bill.

這回你不用花錢，我來付帳。

⑤ YOU'RE MY GUEST.

你是我的客人。

（可以用這句話，讓以上的這些例句聽起來更加友善）

例 Oh, I can't let you pay. It's my treat. You're my guest.

喔，我不能讓你付帳。我請客，你是我的客人。

◇◇◇ 小心陷阱 ◇◇◇

☹ 錯誤用法

I take care of the bill.

我付帳。

☺ 正確用法

I'll take care of the bill.

我付帳。

4.2 分開付帳 Each Person Pays for His/Her Own

BIZ必通句型

❶ LET'S GO DUTCH.

我們各付各的。

例 You paid last night, and I paid this morning. So, let's go Dutch this time.

昨晚你付帳，今天早上我付帳。所以，這回讓我們各付各的。

❷ DUTCH TREAT.

各付各的。

例 Shall we go eat dinner now? Dutch treat.

我們是不是現在去吃晚餐？各付各的。

例 That was a delicious meal. Oh, don't pay the bill again.
It's Dutch treat, okay?

這餐實在美味。喔，別又付帳。這回各付各的，好嗎？

❸ SPLIT THE BILL.

帳單分開算。

（這個說法是用在帳單只有一張，但是每個人只付自己點的食物時）

例 Since we are going Dutch, we can ask the cashier to split
the bill.

因為我們各付各的，我們可以要求櫃檯把帳單分開算。

例 The food was great but quite expensive. There is no
need for just one person to pay. Let's just split the bill.

食物實在美味，不過相當貴。沒有必要光要一個人付錢，讓我們
把帳單分開算吧。

Show Time

A: That was a great meal.

B: Yes, it sure was.

A: How much is it?

B: It's on me.

A: No. No, I'll pay for my own. Let's go Dutch.

B: Really, it's on me.

A: Well, thanks.

A：這頓飯實在很棒！

B：是啊，的確如此。

A：這一頓要多少錢？

B：我請客。

A：不，不，我付我自己的部分。讓我們各付各的。

B：真的，我請客。

A：喔，謝了。

5 觀察客人 Monitoring the Guest

　　有些特殊的英文用語可以讓你表達對客人的需求和期望的關心。這種用語叫做觀察用語。

5.1 確認客人的狀況 Checking the Guest's Status

BIZ必通句型

❶ IS EVERYTHING OKAY?
一切都還好嗎？

❷ IS EVERYTHING ALRIGHT?
一切都還好嗎？

❸ CAN I GET YOU ANYTHING ELSE?
我可以幫你拿些什麼嗎？

❹ IS THERE ANYTHING YOU NEED?
你需要些什麼東西嗎？

❺ IS THERE ANYTHING I CAN GET YOU?
我可以幫你拿些什麼東西嗎？

❻ IS THERE ANYTHING I CAN DO TO MAKE YOUR STAY MORE COMFORTABLE?
我可以幫你作些什麼好讓你停留的這段時間更舒適？

5.2 注意特定的需求 Paying Attention to Specific Needs

BIZ必通句型

❶ 客人看起來不舒服時

YOU DON'T LOOK WELL. WOULD YOU LIKE TO...?

你看起來不舒服，你想不想……？

例 You don't look well. Would you like to go back to the hotel and take a rest?

你看起來不舒服。要不要回旅館休息？

例 You don't look well. Would you like to see a doctor?

你看起來不舒服。要不要看醫生？

❷ 客人似乎很無聊時

1) IF YOU'RE NOT HAVING FUN, WE CAN...

如果你玩得不開心，我們可以……

例 If you're not having fun, we can go somewhere else.

如果你玩得不開心，我們可以去別的地方。

例 If you're not having fun, we can go to a disco.

如果你玩得不開心，我們可以去迪斯可。

2) IF THIS ISN'T INTERESTING, WE CAN...

如果這沒有意思的話，我們可以……

例 If this isn't interesting, we can try a pub.

如果這沒有意思的話，我們可以去酒館。

例 If this isn't interesting, we can go to a museum instead.

如果這沒有意思的話，我們可以改去博物館。

❸ 客人似乎不喜歡某些事情
IF YOU DON'T LIKE..., WE CAN...
如果你不喜歡……，我們可以……
例 If you don't like the food, we can eat something else.
如果你不喜歡這食物，我們可以吃些別的。
例 If you don't like this place, we can go to another restaurant.
如果你不喜歡這個地方，我們可以去另外一家餐廳。

❹ 客人似乎對某樣東西沒什麼興趣時
IF YOU WOULD PREFER SOMETHING ELSE, WE CAN...
如果你比較喜歡別的，我們可以……
例 If you would prefer something else, we can try other flavors.
如果你比較喜歡別的，我們可以試試別的口味。
例 If you would prefer something else, we can go to a different place.
如果你比較喜歡別的，我們可以到別的地方。

❺ 客人對作某件事沒有興趣時
IF YOU WOULD PREFER TO DO SOMETHING ELSE, WE CAN...
如果你比較想做別的事情，我們可以……
例 If you would prefer to do something else, we can take a walk along the river.
如果你比較想做別的事情，我們可以去河邊散步。
例 If you would prefer to do something else, we can go see the night view.
如果你比較想做別的事情，我們可以去看夜景。

Show Time

❶ Guest : The food is great.

Host   : I'm glad you like it. Is there anything else I can get you?

Guest : No, thanks. I am really full!

客人：食物很棒。

主人：我很高興你喜歡。我還可以再幫你點些什麼嗎？

客人：不了，謝謝。我真的很飽！

❷ Guest : There are a lot of seafood restaurants on this street. Is there only seafood here?

Host   : Mostly seafood. If you would prefer something else, we can go to a European restaurant.

Guest : Well, that would be better for me because I am not used to seafood.

Host   : It's no problem. Let's go to the European restaurant.

客人：這條街上有好多海鮮餐廳。這兒是不是只有海鮮？

主人：大多是海鮮。如果你偏好別的，我們可以去一家歐洲餐廳。

客人：喔，那對我比較好，因為我不習慣吃海鮮。

主人：沒問題。我們就去這家歐洲餐廳吧！

Remember the Principles

1 交際和接待客人最重要的就是要設身處地為訪客著想。

The most important part of socializing and entertaining is to put yourself in the shoes of the visitor.

2 盡可能地了解你的訪客,這樣你才知道哪種餐廳以及其他哪些地方是邀請客人的最好選擇。

Learn as much as possible about your visitor so that you will know what kind of restaurants and other places are the best choices for making invitations.

Word list

put oneself in another's shoes 站在別人的立場想

6 實戰演練　Partner Practice

依據下列情境，找個同伴一起模擬對話，作為實戰前的演練。

❶ A與B兩人在洽商會議後私下聊天。A是台灣人，B是外國人。A
想和這位外國客人一起作些娛樂。

1) A：提出去某處的邀請（一個地方，沒有其他的選擇）
   B：接受邀請
2) A：提出去某處的邀請（一個地方，沒有其他的選擇）
   B：拒絕這個邀請
3) A：提出去別處的邀請，並提供選擇
   B：接受邀請
4) A：提出去別處的邀請，並提供選擇
   B：拒絕邀請

❷ A和B剛到達餐廳，在他們的位置坐定。A是台灣人，B是外國
人。

1) A：問要不要吃點東西或是來點飲料
   B：同意
2) B：告訴A食物聞起來很香，並且詢問多少錢
   A：告訴B你請客
3) B：提議各付各的
   A：告訴B你會請客
4) A：看看B的反應
   B：自行決定如何回應

TWO

正式溝通的模式

Formal Communication Formats

商場上的溝通需要正式的用語。需要使用正式英文的洽商場合有五個：電話、簡報、舉行會議、談判以及帶領訪客參觀公司。這個部分提供使各位有能力應付這些場合所需的關鍵英文用語。在下面的五章中，各位即將學習到的英文技巧會讓你在正式的商業溝通中更有信心、且有能力去應對。

Business communication requires formal language. There are five business situations that use formal English: telephoning, giving presentations, holding meetings, engaging in negotiations, and conducting company tours. This section provides all the core English you need to be competent in these situations. The English skills that can be learned in the following five chapters will give you confidence and true ability at formal business communication.

第 4 章

打電話
Telephoning

　　用英文講電話要比面對面用英文對話困難。在面對面的進行溝通時，你會獲得許多視覺上的資訊（主要是肢體語言和臉部的表情），幫助你了解對方。不過講電話也有其有利的一面！它的好處是商務電話有其可循的模式以及可以掌握的字彙。當你熟悉這些模式和字彙時，打商務電話就會像騎腳踏車一樣地那般自然。

　　Speaking English on the telephone is more difficult than speaking English face to face. In face to face communication, you have a lot of visual input to help you understand the other person, primarily body language and facial expressions. But there is good news about telephoning! The good news is that business telephoning has predictable patterns and predictable vocabulary. When you become familiar with these patterns and vocabulary, making business phone calls will become natural for you — just like riding a bicycle!

1 電話用語的介紹　Talking about Telephoning

　　在你學習講電話的技巧之前，需要先知道一些基本的字彙。這些基本的字彙在你講電話的時候能發揮很大的功用。

1.1 基本字彙　Basic Vocabulary

　　請試著背下這些字彙。

BIZ必通字彙

電話的部分 (Telephones)
❶ keypad〔`ki,pæd〕 n. 鍵盤　❷ handset〔`hænd,sɛt〕 n. 聽筒
❸ earpiece〔`ɪr,pis〕 n. 受話口
❹ mouthpiece〔`maʊθ,pis〕 n. 送話口

人 (People)
❶ caller〔`kɔlɚ〕 n. 打電話的人
❷ operator〔`ɑpə,retɚ〕 n. 接線生（總機）

通話類型 (Types of Calls)
❶ local call〔`lokḷ `kɔl〕 n. 本地電話
❷ long distance call〔`lɔŋ `dɪstəns `kɔl〕 n. 長途電話
❸ international call〔͵ɪntɚ`næʃənḷ `kɔl〕 n. 國際電話
❹ collect call〔kə`lɛkt `kɔl〕 n. 對方付費電話

打電話的動作 (Call Actions)
❶ answer〔`ænsɚ〕 v. 接（電話）
❷ hang up〔`hæŋ `ʌp〕 v. 掛斷

③ pick up〔`pɪk`ʌp〕 v. 拿起
④ put down〔`pʊt`daʊn〕 v. 放下
⑤ hold〔hold〕 v. 等候
⑥ transfer〔træns`fɝ〕 v. 轉
⑦ put through〔`pʊt`θru〕 v. 轉接
⑧ connect〔kə`nɛkt〕 v. 接通
⑨ forward〔`fɔrwəd〕 v. 轉
⑩ write down〔`raɪt`daʊn〕 v. 寫下
⑪ take down〔`tek`daʊn〕 v. 記下

線路的問題 (Line Problems)
❶ bad line〔`bæd`laɪn〕 n. 線路不良
❷ static〔`stætɪk〕 n. 靜電干擾；雜音
❸ cut off〔`kʌt`ɔf〕 v. 斷線

電話號碼 (Phone Numbers)
❶ extension〔ɪk`stɛnʃən〕 n. 分機
❷ (city, area, country) code〔kod〕 n.（城市、區域、國家）碼

1.2 配合情境的字彙　Vocabulary in Context

　　以完整的句子來說明字彙是很重要的，這樣你才能夠了解如何運用這些字彙。以下範例包含本章開頭所介紹的所有字彙。

　　大聲朗頌每個句子至少一次，是準備運用這些字彙的好辦法。你複頌得愈多次，這些句型在你腦海就烙印得愈久。當情況需要時，這些句型自動會浮上心頭，讓你可以代換其中的字彙，說出漂亮的英語。

1.2a 有關「電話」的字彙 'Telephones' Vocabulary

Show Time

❶ Please enter your credit card number on the **keypad**.
請在電話鍵盤上輸入你信用卡的號碼。

❷ This **handset** is stylish but a bit too small.
這個聽筒很時髦,可是有點太小了。

❸ I hear a strange noise every time I make a call. Maybe there is something wrong with the **earpiece**.
每次我打電話都會聽到奇怪的雜音。電話的收話口可能有問題。

❹ Please speak directly into the **mouthpiece** so the person on the line can hear you clearly.
請直接對著送話口說話,這樣電話線另外一端的人才可以清晰地聽到你的話。

1.2b 有關「人」的字彙 'People' Vocabulary

Show Time

❶ There is a **caller** for Mr. Belmont on line four.
四線有人來電找貝爾蒙先生。(貝爾蒙先生四線電話。)

❷ I need to call the **operator** to ask for assistance in calling our buyer in Germany.
我得打給總機要求協助打電話給我們在德國的買主。

1.2c 有關「線路問題」的字彙 'Line Problems' Vocabulary

Show Time

❶ It is difficult to hear you. I think we have a **bad line**. Let's hang up, and I will call you back.

我很難聽清楚你說什麼，我想線路有問題。我們先掛斷，我再打給你。

❷ There is a lot of **static** on the line. It is difficult to understand you.

這個線路上有很多雜音。很難聽懂你說的話。

❸ I tried to transfer the call, but I accidentally **cut off** the caller. Let me call her back.

我試圖把電話轉過去，但是卻意外地把線掛斷了。讓我再打給她。

❹ Sorry, I got **cut off**. I am on my cell phone, and I drove into a tunnel.

對不起，剛剛線路斷了。我是用手機講電話，剛才剛好開車進隧道。

1.2d 有關「通話類型」的字彙 'Types of Calls' Vocabulary

Show Time

❶ You can use my phone if it is just a **local call**.

如果只是市內電話，你可以用我的電話。

❷ Calling me in Taichung is a **long distance call** since you are in Taipei, so please let me call you instead.

因為你人在台北，打到台中給我是長途電話，所以還是讓我打給你好了。

③ Our department has many customers in Europe, so we make many **international calls** every day.
我們部門有許多歐洲的客戶，所以我們每天都會打許多國際電話。

④ My parents like to talk to me a lot, so they ask me to **call** them **collect**.
我的父母非常喜歡和我講話，所以他們要我打對方付費的電話給他們。

⑤ If you use my phone to call long distance, please make a **collect call**.
如果你用我的電話打長途電話，請以對方付費的方式打。

1.2e 有關「打電話動作」的字彙 'Call Actions' Vocabulary

Show Time

① The phone has rung five times. Someone please **answer** it!
電話已經響了五次。拜託，哪個人去接接電話！

② I know you are angry, but please don't **hang up**!
我知道你很生氣，不過請不要掛斷！

③ It is easy! Just **pick up** the phone and dial the number.
很簡單！只要拿起電話撥號碼就可以了。

❹ Let me see if I can find that information for you. I will **put down** the phone for a few minutes while I search. Is that okay?

我看看能不能幫你找到這個資訊。我在找的時候會暫時把電話放下來，這樣可以嗎？

❺ Mr. Chou is talking with someone right now. Can you **hold** for a minute?

周先生現在正在和別人談話。你可不可以在線上等一會兒？

❻ Yes, Miss Jenkins is available. Let me **transfer** you to her.

是的，珍金斯小姐現在可以接電話。讓我把你轉給她。

❼ You want to speak to Edward? Alright, I will **put** you **through**.

你要跟艾德華說話嗎？好的，我會幫你轉過去。

❽ Mr. Lee is free. Let me **connect** you.

李先生有空。讓我幫你轉接。

❾ The president is at home today, but I know he really wants to speak to you. Let me **forward** your call to his home.

總裁今天在家，不過我知道他真的想和你說話。讓我把你的電話轉到他家。

❿ You would like to leave a message? Okay. Just a moment. Let me **write** it **down**.

你要留言？好的，等一下。讓我把留言記下來。

⑪ You want to order some products from our catalog? Great. I am ready to **take down** the information for your order.

你想要訂購我們目錄裡的一些產品？好極了，我已經準備好記下有關你的訂單的資料。

1.2f 有關「電話號碼」的字彙 'Phone Numbers' Vocabulary

(Show Time)

❶ Just call my office, then dial **extension** 541. That is my office phone.

打電話到我辦公室，然後撥分機541就行了。那是我辦公室的電話。

❷ I need to call our client in Indonesia. Does anybody know the **country code**?

我得打電話給我們印尼的客戶。有沒有人知道印尼的國碼？

❸ I am looking in the directory, but I can't find the **city code** for Frankfurt.

我正在查電話簿，不過找不到法蘭克福的市碼。

❹ We have many customers in different cities in America. We have to keep a list of all the **area codes** of these cities.

我們在美國各大城市有許多客戶。我們必須留一份列出所有這些城市區域碼的清單。

Word list

Indonesia〔ˌɪndo`niʃə〕 n. 印尼共和國  Frankfurt〔`fræŋkfət〕 n. 法蘭克福

2 電話洽商的基本步驟
Basic Parts of Making a Business Phone Call

你得熟悉打電話的基本步驟。以下列舉出最常見的幾個部分。這些不是打電話的所有環節。有些電話的環節比較少，有些則比較多。不過如果你了解了這些基本的環節，幾乎所有類型的電話你都能相當純熟地應對。

基本的環節包括：

1. 自我介紹
2. 要求和某人談話
3. 說明打電話的目的
4. 開始對話
5. 說明主要的訊息
6. 摘要說明
7. 總結

★★★ *BIZ* 一點通 ★★★

第二個部分（要求和某人談話）以及第三個部分（說明打電話的目的）的順序有時候可以倒過來。

這七個步驟將會在 2.1 到 2.7 當中加以說明。各位不需要背下所有的例句，因為沒有這個必要，而且這麼做可能令你在實際運用時更加困惑。當各位在唸這些例句時，只需注意句型以及用語即可。最好的辦法就是從以下部分選擇一兩個適合你個性、風格或是你工作環境背景的範例，反覆練習直到這些句子烙印在你腦海為止。

2.1 自我介紹 Introducing Yourself

自我介紹的基本模式是：姓名＋職稱＋公司。雖然每次自我介紹可

能都有些不同，不過這是最常見的模式。其實許多時候無須報上自己的
職稱，特別是對方已經知道你是何方神聖的情況下更是如此。

自我介紹的方法有幾種。記住，只要挑一兩個句型記住就可以。每
次打電話的時候，這些句型就成了你個人運用的風格。

BIZ必通句型

❶ THIS IS...OF...

我是……的……

例 Hello. This is Kevin Costner of Triple C Cable Company.

哈囉。我是 Triple C 電纜公司的凱文‧克斯納。

❷ THIS IS...CALLING FROM...

我是從……打來的……

例 Good morning. This is Betty Davis calling from Beta
Multimedia.

早安。我是從貝塔多媒體打來的貝蒂‧戴維斯。

❸ THIS IS... I AM CALLING FROM...

我是……，我是從……打來的。

例 Hello. This is Candice Bergan. I am calling from Paris
Clothiers.

哈囉。我是甘迪斯‧伯根，我是從巴黎服飾打來的。

❹ THIS IS..., A/THE...AT...

我是……，……的……

例 Hi. This is Robert DeNiro, a sales assistant at Zeta
Computers.

嗨，我是勞伯‧迪尼諾，我是 Zeta 電腦公司的業務助理。

❺ THIS IS... (name), ... (name)'S...AT... (company)

我是……（人名），……（公司）……（人名）的……

例 Good afternoon. This is Hillary Clinton, President Wu's Assistant at Super Semiconductors.

午安，我是希拉蕊‧柯林頓，超級半導體公司吳總裁的助理。

◇◇◇ 小心陷阱 ◇◇◇

☹ 錯誤用法

This is Jane **call** from Lion Coffee Makers.

我是從里昂咖啡製造公司打來的珍。

☺ 正確用法

This is Jane **calling** from Lion Coffee Makers.

我是從里昂咖啡製造公司打來的珍。

2.2 要求和某人談話 Asking for Someone

❶ ..., PLEASE.

請接……

例 Mr. Pitt, please.

請接彼特先生。

❷ IS...IN?

……在嗎？

例 Is Mrs. Baker in?

貝克太太在嗎？

Word list

semiconductor〔͵sɛmɪkənˋdʌktə〕 *n.* 半導體

❸ IS...AVAILABLE?

……在嗎？

例 Is Ms. Margaret available?

瑪格莉特女士有空嗎？

❹ MAY I SPEAK TO...?

我可以和……講話嗎？

例 May I speak to Miss Peterson?

我可以和彼得森小姐講話嗎？

❺ COULD I SPEAK TO...?

我可以和……講話嗎？

例 Could I speak to Mary Anderson?

我可以和瑪莉・安德森講話嗎？

Show Time

Receiver : Hello. Taiwan Turbo Company.

Caller   : Hi. This is Jason Argonaut of Greek Shipping. Is Alan Wu in?

Receiver : Yes. Just a moment.

Caller   : Thanks.

接電話者：哈囉，台灣 Turbo 公司。

打電話者：嗨，我是希臘船運公司的傑森・阿格納。請問亞倫・吳在嗎？

接電話者：在，請等一下。

打電話者：謝謝。

2.2a 不知道對方姓名的情況

Asking for Someone Whose Name is Not Known

當我們打電話的時候，有時候我們並不知道要找哪一個部門、分機號碼、或是哪一個人。以下這些用語可以協助各位應付這樣的情況。

BIZ必通句型

❶ COULD YOU CONNECT ME WITH THE PERSON WHO...?

你能幫我轉給……的人嗎？

例 Could you connect me with the person who is in charge of overseas orders, please?

能請您幫我轉給負責海外訂單的人嗎？

例 Could you connect me with the person who answers product inquiries?

你能幫我轉給負責回覆產品詢問的人嗎？

❷ COULD I HAVE THE PERSON WHO...?

我可以找……的人談話嗎？

例 Could I have the person who handles U.S. accounts?

我可以找負責美國客戶的人談話嗎？

例 Could I have the person who is responsible for your wine promotion?

我可以找你們負責酒類推廣的人談話嗎？

ord list

in charge of〔ɪn `tʃɑrdʒ əv〕 *prep.* 負責（管理、照顧）……

❸ **COULD I TALK WITH THE PERSON WHO...?**

我可以和……的人談嗎？

例 Could I talk with the person who takes Asian orders?

我可以和接亞洲訂單的人談話嗎？

例 Could I talk with the person who takes care of Internet questions?

我可以和負責處理網路問題的人談話嗎？

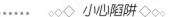
◇◇◇ 小心陷阱 ◇◇◇

☹ 錯誤用法

Could I have **the selling clocks person**?

我可以找銷售時鐘的人談嗎？

☺ 正確用法

Could I have **the person who sells clocks**?

我可以找銷售時鐘的人談嗎？

2.2b 要求轉接對方分機 Asking for an Extension

BIZ 必通句型

❶ **EXTENSION..., PLEASE.**

請接……號分機

例 Extension 215, please.

請接215號分機。

❷ **COULD I HAVE EXTENSION...?**

可以幫我轉……號分機嗎？

例 Could I have extension 7114?

可以幫我轉7114號分機嗎？

❸ **COULD YOU CONNECT ME WITH EXTENSION...?**

你能幫我接……號分機嗎？

例 Could you connect me with extension 701?

你能幫我接701號分機嗎？

❹ **COULD YOU PUT ME THROUGH TO EXTENSION...?**

你能幫我接……號分機嗎？

例 Could you put me through to extension 282?

你能幫我接282號分機嗎？

❺ **I'D LIKE EXTENSION..., PLEASE.**

請轉……號分機。

例 I'd like extension 45, please.

請轉45號分機。

◇◇◇ 小心陷阱 ◇◇◇

☹ 錯誤用法

Could you connect me extension 901?

您能幫我接分機901嗎？

☺ 正確用法

Could you connect me **with** extension 901?

您能幫我接分機901嗎？

2.2c 要求轉接到某個部門或是辦公室 Asking for a Department or Office

*BIZ*必通句型

❶ **THE...DEPARTMENT/OFFICE, PLEASE.**

請轉……部門／辦公室。

例 The Customer Service Department, please.
請轉客戶服務部。

例 The President's Office, please.
請轉總裁辦公室。

❷ **COULD I HAVE THE...DEPARTMENT/OFFICE?**
可以幫我轉……部門／辦公室嗎？

例 Could I have the Public Relations Department?
可以幫我轉公關部門嗎？

例 Could I have the Personnel Office?
可以幫我轉人事部嗎？

❸ **COULD YOU CONNECT ME WITH THE...
DEPARTMENT/OFFICE?**
您能幫我接……部門／辦公室嗎？

例 Could you connect me with the Finance Department?
您能幫我接財務部門嗎？

例 Could you connect me with the director's office?
您能幫我接主任辦公室嗎？

❹ **COULD YOU PUT ME THROUGH TO THE...
DEPARTMENT/OFFICE?**
您能幫我轉接……部門／辦公室嗎？

例 Could you put me through to your manager's office,
please?
您能幫我轉接經理辦公室嗎？

❺ **I'D LIKE THE...DEPARTMENT/OFFICE, PLEASE.**
請幫我轉……部門／辦公室。

例 I'd like the Accounting Department, please.
請幫我轉會計部門。

2.3 說明致電的目的 Stating the Purpose of the Call

BIZ必通句型

❶ I AM CALLING TO... (+ verb)
我打電話來是為了……（動詞）
例 I am calling to set up an appointment with Mr. Dreiling.
我打電話來是為了和得瑞林先生約碰面的時間。
例 I am calling to find out about your new product, the AZ501.
我打電話來是為了想了解你們的新產品 AZ501。

❷ I AM CALLING ABOUT... (+ noun)
我打電話來討論關於……（名詞）
例 I am calling about your recent product catalog.
我打電話來討論你們最新的產品目錄。
例 I am calling about my visit to your company next week.
我打電話來討論下周拜訪你們公司的相關事宜。

❸ I AM CALLING TO LET YOU KNOW...
我打電話來讓您知道……
例 I am calling to let you know that I am available for a meeting next week.
我打電話來讓您知道我下個禮拜可以來開會。

Word list

available〔ə`veləbḷ〕 *adj.* 有空的；可用的

④ THE REASON I AM CALLING IS...

我打電話來的原因是……

例 The reason I am calling is to invite you to our opening ceremony on Friday.

我打電話來的原因是為了邀請您週五參加我們的開幕典禮。

⑤ THE PURPOSE OF MY CALL IS TO... (+ verb)

我打電話來的目的是……（動詞）

例 The purpose of my call is to let you know we have a new product available.

我打電話來的目的是讓您知道我們有一項新產品。

例 The purpose of my call is to ask you about an order you placed last month.

我打電話來的目的是要問有關上個月您下的訂單。

◇◇ 小心陷阱 ◇◇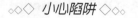

☹ 錯誤用法

I am **call** to talk to Bob.

我打電話來是要和鮑伯說話。

☺ 正確用法

I am **calling** to talk to Bob.

我打電話來是要和鮑伯說話。

Show Time

❶ Receiver : Mega Computers. May I help you?

Caller　　: Yes.　This is Martin Short of Kansas Shoes.
　　　　　　 Could I have the person who is in charge of your international accounts?

Receiver : Sure.　Can you hold for a moment?

Caller　　: Yes, thank you.

接電話者：Mega 電腦公司。我可以為您服務嗎？
打電話者：是的。這裡是堪薩斯皮鞋公司的馬丁‧梭特。我可以和
　　　　　貴公司負責國際客戶的人員談話嗎？
接電話者：當然。您可以等一下嗎？
打電話者：可以，謝謝。

❷ Receiver : Penny Silverware. Can I help you?
Caller　　 : Yes. This is Steve Martin of Missouri
　　　　　　 Motorcycles. I am calling to speak with your
　　　　　　 marketing director.
Receiver : Alright. Let me put you through.
Caller　　 : Thank you.

接電話者：潘妮銀器公司。我可以為您服務嗎？
打電話者：是的，我是密蘇里機車公司的史蒂夫‧馬丁。我打電話
　　　　　來想找貴公司的行銷部主任談話。
接電話者：好的。讓我為您轉接。
打電話者：謝謝。

2.4 打開話題 Opening a Conversation

　　以下用語很適合用來打開話題，然後再進入洽商的主題。簡短的對
話當中，雙方可能各自只說幾句話而已。這端視你和對方的情況而定，

Word list

silverware〔`sɪlvə‚wɛr〕 n. 銀器

譬如：心情、個人風格等等，需要自己善加判斷。

BIZ必通句型

❶ HOW ARE THINGS?
情況如何？
例 How are things there in Paris?
在巴黎情況如何？
例 How are things at your new office?
你在新辦公室的情況如何？

❷ HOW IS/ARE...?
……怎麼樣？
例 How is the weather there?
那邊的天氣怎麼樣？
例 How is your new office?
你的新辦公室怎麼樣？
例 How are the products you ordered last time?
你上次訂購的產品怎麼樣？

❸ I HOPE YOU HAD A NICE...
我希望你有個美好的……
例 I hope you had a nice weekend.
希望您上週末很愉快。
例 I hope you had a nice exhibition in London last month.
希望您上個月在倫敦的展覽很順利。

❹ I HEARD...
我聽說……
例 I heard the weather is very cold there recently.
我聽說那邊最近天氣很冷。

例 I heard your new product is selling very well.
我聽說你們的新產品賣得很好。

例 I heard about the forest fire in your state. Is everything okay?
我聽說了你們那州的森林大火。一切都還好嗎？

Show Time

Receiver : Yang Ming Flowers.

Caller : Hi. This is Elly Andrews of the Taipei Hilton. I am calling about our recent flower order.

Receiver : Oh, Elly. This is Tim. I haven't talked to you in a while. How are things at the Hilton?

Caller : Everything is just fine, thanks. I heard the weather has been great up on the mountain there.

Receiver : Yes, it has been wonderful. Anyway, how can I help you?

- -

接電話者：陽明花圃。

打電話者：嗨。我是台北希爾頓的艾莉‧安德魯斯。我打電話來想討論我們最近訂的花。

接電話者：喔，艾莉。我是提姆，有一陣子沒和妳聯絡了。希爾頓那邊情況如何？

打電話者：一切都很好，謝謝。我聽說山上的天氣一直很好。

接電話者：是的，一直都很棒。有何我可以效勞的地方嗎？

2.5 說明關鍵的資訊 Stating Key Information

關鍵的資訊通常包括數字，如：數據、日期、時間、貨幣等。以下這個部分的重點在於數字的相關資訊：

日期的表達方式是有彈性的，下列這些說法都可以接受：

Monday, May 5th, at 5 o'clock p.m.	五月五日，禮拜一，下午五點鐘
Monday, May 5th, at 5 p.m.	五月五日，禮拜一，下午五點鐘
Monday, the 5th of May, at 5 p.m.	五月五日，禮拜一，下午五點鐘
5 o'clock p.m. on Monday, May 5th	五月五日，禮拜一下午五點鐘
5 p.m. on Monday, May 5th	五月五日，禮拜一下午五點鐘
5 p.m. on Monday, the 5th of May	五月五日，禮拜一下午五點鐘

貨幣數字表達的方式也很有彈性，以下這些說法都可以接受：

500 U.S. dollars	美金五百元——這種說法最常見
500 dollars, U.S.	美金五百元
U.S. 500 dollars	美金五百元
2,500 NT dollars	新台幣兩千五百元——這種說法最爲常見
2,500 dollars, N.T.	新台幣兩千五百元
N.T. 2,500 dollars	新台幣兩千五百元

◇◇◇ 小心陷阱 ◇◇◇

☹ 錯誤用法

It costs three **hundreds** dollars.

這要美金三百元。

☺ 正確用法

It costs three **hundred** dollars.

這要美金三百元。

BIZ必通句型

❶ I WOULD LIKE TO MAKE AN APPOINTMENT FOR...

我要約……

例 I would like to make an appointment for next Thursday, June the 9th, at 4:30.

我要約下個禮拜四，六月九日四點半。

◇◇◇ 小心陷阱 ◇◇◇

☹ 錯誤用法

I like to make an appointment for next week.

我想要約下個禮拜。

☺ 正確用法

I **would** like to make an appointment for next week.

我想要約下個禮拜。

❷ COULD I MAKE AN APPOINTMENT FOR...?

我可不可以約……？

例 Could I make an appointment for Friday, the 21st of February?

我可不可以約禮拜五，二月二十一日？

❸ WOULD/WILL...BE AVAILABLE AT/ON...?

……有沒有空？

例 Would Blake be available on Wednesday at 10 a.m.?

布萊克禮拜三早上十點有沒有空？

例 Would Janice be available at 2:00 this afternoon?

珍妮絲今天下午兩點鐘有沒有空？

例 Will you be available next Tuesday at 4 p.m.?

你下個禮拜二下午四點鐘有沒有空？

◇◇◇ 小心陷阱 ◇◇◇

☹ 錯誤用法

You should arrive **at** Wednesday.

你應該禮拜三到。

☺ 正確用法

You should arrive **on** Wednesday.

你應該禮拜三到。

❹ **YOU ARE SCHEDULED FOR...**

你被排在……

例 You are scheduled for 2:30 p.m. on Thursday, the 5th of March.

你被排在三月五日，禮拜四下午兩點半。

❺ **...WILL COST...**

……要花……

例 Your order will cost 300,000 NT dollars.

你訂的貨要三十萬台幣。

例 That will cost 10,500 U.S. dollars.

那要一萬五百美元。

❻ **THE COST OF...IS...**

……的費用為……

例 The cost of one dozen cameras is 144,000 NT dollars.

十二台照相機的價錢為十四萬四千台幣。

例 The cost of our shoes is U.S. 75 dollars per pair.
我們鞋子的價錢為每雙七十五塊美金。

2.6 摘要說明打電話的重點 Summarizing

在講電話的時候，可能會聽錯、寫錯、或是誤會對方講的話。所以，洽商電話快要接近尾聲時，應該重新概要說明剛才談話的重點或是對方所說的重點。如果電話上雙方交換了許多複雜的資訊，可以每談到一個段落，就稍微停下來作個總結，而不是等到快要談完的時候才對整個對話進行總結。

BIZ必通句型

❶ **I WOULD LIKE TO GO OVER...**
   我想要回頭重複一下⋯⋯
   例 Before I go, I would like to go over the main points. We have agreed to...
   在離開之前，我想要回頭重複一下主要重點。我們已經同意⋯⋯

❷ **WHY DON'T WE GO OVER...AGAIN.**
   我們何不再查看⋯⋯一遍。
   例 Your order is pretty big. Why don't we go over it again.
   您的訂單很大。我們何不再查看一遍。

❸ **I WOULD LIKE TO REPEAT...**
   我想要重複說明⋯⋯
   例 Before I go, I would like to repeat the meeting date. It will be next week on Monday at 2:30 p.m.
   在離開之前，我想要重複一次會議的日期。會議將在下個禮拜一下午兩點半舉行。

❹ LET ME REPEAT THAT, OKAY?

讓我再重複一次,好嗎?

例 Let me repeat that, okay? You said there is a 10% discount on every purchase of 200 pieces or more.

讓我再重複一次,好嗎?你說每次購買兩百個或兩百個以上可以有百分之十的折扣。

(注意,當談話內容資訊較多時用「go over」;資訊較少時則用「repeat」。)

❺ LET ME SUMMARIZE./...

讓我作個總結。

例 Let me summarize the information we have talked about, okay?

讓我對我們剛才談到的資訊作個總結,好嗎?

例 We have discussed many details. Let me summarize.

我們已經討論過許多細節。讓我作個總結。

Show Time

Caller : ...The merchandise needs to arrive on Monday, the ninth of August, so that we can load it onto the containers by Wednesday morning.

Receiver : I would like to go over the details again.

Caller : Sure.

Receiver : You are ordering twelve crates of our Foreman Cookers. They must arrive on Monday, August ninth.

Word list

crate〔kret〕 *n.* 板條箱

Caller ：Yes, that's all correct.

打電話者：……這批貨得在八月九日週一到，這樣我們才可以在週
三早上裝上貨櫃。

接電話者：我想要再重複一次細節。

打電話者：沒問題。

接電話者：您訂了十二箱我們的福而滿電鍋。這批貨要在週一，八
月九日到達。

打電話者：是的，完全正確。

2.7 結束談話 Concluding

電話談話進行告一段落時，可以一兩句話來作個結束。模式如下：

1. 你說總結的話
2. 對方也說總結的話
3. 你說再見
4. 對方也說再見

BIZ 必通句型

❶ **I LOOK FORWARD TO...**

我期待……

例 I look forward to seeing you.

我期待和您見面。

例 I look forward to our meeting.

我期待我們的會議。

◇◇◇ 小心陷阱 ◇◇◇

☹ 錯誤用法

I look forward to **see** you.

我期待和您見面。

☺ 正確用法

I look forward to **seeing** you.

我期待和您見面。

❷ THANKS FOR CALLING.

謝謝您打電話來。

❸ THANKS FOR YOUR HELP.

謝謝您的協助。

❹ IT WAS NICE TO TALK WITH YOU.

很高興能和您談話。

❺ I APPRECIATE YOU TALKING WITH ME.

我很感激您和我談話。

❻ THAT'S ALL I WANTED TO TALK ABOUT.

我要說的就是這些。

```
·················· ◇◇ 小心陷阱 ◇◇◇ ··················

  ☹ 錯誤用法
    Thanks for your **calling**.
    謝謝您打電話來。
  ☺ 正確用法
    Thanks for your **call**.
    或 Thanks for **calling**.
    謝謝您打電話來。
```

Show Time

❶ Receiver : ...Is there anything else I can help you with?
  Caller　　 : No.　That's all for now. Thanks.
  Receiver : Thanks for calling.
  Caller　　 : No problem.
  Receiver : Bye-bye.
  Caller　　 : Goodbye.

- -

  接電話者：⋯⋯有沒有其他我還可以幫忙的地方？
  打電話者：沒有。目前就這樣，謝謝。
  接電話者：謝謝您打電話來。
  打電話者：不客氣。
  接電話者：再見。
  打電話者：再見。

❷ Receiver : ...We will ship those products immediately.
  Caller　　 : Great.　That's all I wanted to talk about.
  Receiver : Okay.
  Caller　　 : Goodbye.
  Receiver : Bye.

接電話者：…… 我們會立即運送這些貨品。
打電話者：太好了。我就是要講這些。
接電話者：好的。
打電話者：再見。
接電話者：再見。

3 接洽商電話的基本步驟
Basic Parts of Receiving a Business Phone Call

　　各位同樣得熟悉接電話的基本應對。接電話要比打電話容易，因爲打電話的人要負責引導談話方向。接電話最常見的應對方式如下：

1. 接電話
2. 說明身分
3. 詢問對方的身分
4. 詢問對方打電話來的目的
5. 轉接

3.1 接電話 Answering the Phone

BIZ必通句型

接主電話之用語

❶ ... (company)
……（公司）。
例 Taiwan Semiconductor Corporation.
台積電。

❷ HELLO. ... (company)
哈囉，……（公司）。
例 Hello. Taichung Motors.
哈囉，台中汽車公司。

❸ ... (company) MAY I HELP YOU?
……（公司），我可以爲您服務嗎？
例 Beta Computers. May I help you?
Beta 電腦公司。我可以爲您服務嗎？

❹ GOOD MORNING/AFTERNOON/EVENING.
... (company)

早安／午安／晚安，……（公司）。

例 Good afternoon. Taichung Trucking.

午安，台中卡車公司。

例 Good morning. Tainan Tire Company.

早安，台南輪胎公司。

❺ ... (company) HOW MAY I DIRECT YOUR CALL?

……（公司）。請問您電話要轉哪位？

例 Taiwan Beer Company. How may I direct your call?

台灣啤酒公司。請問您電話要轉哪位？

BIZ必通句型

接分機電話的用語

❶ ...OFFICE/DEPARTMENT.

……辦公室／部門。

例 Marketing Department.

行銷部。

例 Budget Director's Office.

預算主任辦公室。

❷ HELLO. THIS IS THE...OFFICE/DEPARTMENT.

哈囉，這裡是……辦公室／部門。

例 Hello. This is the Vice President's Office.

哈囉，這裡是副總裁辦公室。

例 Hello. This is the Loan Department.

哈囉，這裡是貸款部。

❸ CAN/MAY I HELP YOU?

我可以為您服務嗎？

例 Marketing Department. Can I help you?

行銷部，我可以為您服務嗎？

例 Hello. This is the Loan Department. May I help you?

哈囉，這裡是貸款部。我可以為您服務嗎？

3.2 確認身份的說法 Confirming One's Identity

*BIZ*必通句型

❶ THIS IS...

我是……

例 This is Bernard.

我是柏納。

❷ SPEAKING.

我就是。

❸ ...SPEAKING.

我就是……

例 Mrs. Chen speaking.

我就是陳太太。

❹ YOU ARE SPEAKING TO...

我就是……

例 You are speaking to Henry.

我就是亨利。

◇◇◇ 小心陷阱 ◇◇◇

⊗ 錯誤用法

I am Gary Hsu.

我是蓋瑞・徐。

☺ 正確用法

This is Gary Hsu.

我是蓋瑞・徐。

Show Time

❶ Receiver : Good morning. Lion Lazer Company.

Caller　　: Hi. I would like to speak to Lisa, please.

Receiver : This is Lisa.

Caller　　: Hi, Lisa. This is Tom Bradley calling about your recent order.

接電話者：早安，Lion Lazer 公司。

打電話者：嗨，麻煩找麗莎聽電話。

接電話者：我就是麗莎。

打電話者：嗨，麗莎。我是湯姆・布萊德利，我打電話來談您最近下的訂單。

❷ Receiver : Sales Department.

Caller　　: Is Rose available?

Receiver : Speaking.

Caller　　: Rose, this is Jonathan Kipling. I am calling about the bill for our last order.

接電話者：業務部。

打電話者：羅絲在嗎？

接電話者：我就是。

打電話者：羅絲，我是強納森‧克普林。我打電話來談我們上次訂
貨的帳單。

3.3 詢問對方身分的方法 Asking for a Caller's Identity

BIZ必通句型

❶ **WHO IS CALLING, PLEASE?**
請問您是哪位？

❷ **MAY I ASK WHO IS CALLING?**
我可以請問您是哪位嗎？

❸ **MAY I HAVE YOUR NAME?**
請問您的大名？

❹ **MAY I TAKE YOUR NAME?**
我可以知道您的大名嗎？

3.4 詢問打電話的目的 Asking the Purpose of a Call

BIZ必通句型

❶ **MAY I ASK THE PURPOSE OF YOUR CALL?**
我可以請問您打電話來的目的嗎？

❷ **MAY I ASK WHY YOU ARE CALLING?**
我可以請問您為什麼打電話來嗎？

❸ MAY I ASK WHAT YOUR CALL IS REGARDING?
我可以請問您打電話來是要談什麼事情嗎？

❹ MAY I ASK THE REASON FOR YOUR CALL?
我可以請問您打電話來的原因嗎？

◇◇ 小心陷阱 ◇◇

☹ 錯誤用法

May I ask why **are you** calling?
我可以請問您為什麼打電話來嗎？

☺ 正確用法

May I ask why **you are** calling?
我可以請問您為什麼打電話來嗎？

Show Time

Receiver : Good afternoon. Techno Tools.
Caller　　: Yes. I'd like to speak to the production manager.
Receiver : May I ask who is calling?
Caller　　: This is Mike Bettis, the chief buyer at Peace Hospital.
Receiver : Let me see if he is in.

接電話者：午安，Techno 工具公司。
打電話者：您好，我想要和生產部經理談話。
接電話者：可以請教您的大名嗎？
打電話者：我叫麥克‧貝提斯，和平醫院的採購長。
接電話者：讓我看看他在不在。

3.5 轉接電話 Transferring a Call

BIZ必通句型

❶ I'LL PUT YOU THROUGH (TO THE...).
我會幫您轉接（給……）。
例 I'll put you through to the Sales Department.
我會幫您轉接給業務部。

❷ LET ME PUT YOU THROUGH (TO THE...).
讓我幫您轉接（給……）。
例 Let me put you through to the Sales Department.
讓我幫您轉接給業務部。

❸ I'LL CONNECT YOU (TO THE...).
我會幫您接（給……）。
例 I'll connect you to the manager's office.
我會幫您接經理辦公室。

❹ LET ME CONNECT YOU (TO THE...).
讓我幫您接（給……）。
例 Let me connect you to the manager's office.
讓我幫您接經理辦公室。

❺ I'LL TRANSFER YOU (TO THE...).
我會幫您轉（給……）。
例 I'll transfer you to the production plant.
我會幫您轉給生產工廠。

❻ LET ME TRANSFER YOU (TO THE...).

讓我幫您轉（給……）。

例 Let me transfer you to the production plant.

讓我幫您轉給生產工廠。

❼ JUST A MOMENT.

請等一下。

例 Just a moment. I'll connect you.

請等一下，我會幫您轉接。

例 Just a moment. Let me put you through.

請等一下，讓我幫您轉接。

◇◇◇ 小心陷阱 ◇◇◇

☹ 錯誤用法

I transfer you.

我幫您轉接。

☺ 正確用法

I **will** transfer you.

我幫您轉接。

Show Time

Receiver : Good morning. Kelvin Knife Company. May I help you?

Caller : Hello. This is Jennifer Connaly of Ace Cardboard Company. Could you connect me with the shipping department?

Receiver : May I ask the purpose of your call?

Caller : I'd like to see if our latest order has been loaded onto the trucks yet.

Receiver : Alright, I'll transfer you.

接電話者：早安，凱文刀具公司。我可以為您服務嗎？

打電話者：哈囉，我是王牌紙版公司的珍妮佛‧康納利。您可以幫我轉接給貨運部嗎？

接電話者：可以請問您打電話的目的嗎？

打電話者：我想查詢我們最新訂的貨是否已經裝上卡車。

接電話者：好的，我會幫您轉接。

4 打電話常見的狀況 Common Phoning Situations

各位還應知道一些其他情況所需的英文電話用語，這些情況包括：
1. 分機忙線中
2. 某人無法接聽電話
3. 釐清

4.1 分機忙線中 Busy Extension

4.1a 告知分機忙線中 Saying the Extension Is Busy

*BIZ*必通句型

❶ THE LINE IS BUSY.
線路忙線中。

❷ THE EXTENSION IS BUSY.
分機忙線中。

❸ ...IS ON THE LINE.
……正在講電話。
例 Mrs. Hayden is on the line.
賀登女士正在講電話。

4.1b 詢問打電話的人打算怎麼辦 Asking the Caller What to Do

BIZ必通句型

❶ WOULD YOU LIKE TO HOLD?

您要等待嗎？

❷ CAN YOU HOLD?

您可否等一下？

❸ WOULD YOU LIKE TO CALL BACK?

您要再打過來嗎？

❹ CAN YOU CALL BACK?

您可以再打過來嗎？

❺ WOULD YOU LIKE TO WAIT UNTIL THE LINE IS FREE?

您要等到線路通嗎？

◇◇ 小心陷阱 ◇◇

☹ 錯誤用法

Could you like to hold?

您要等待嗎？

☺ 正確用法

Would you like to hold?

您要等待嗎？

Show Time

Receiver : Huey Packford Company. May I help you?
Caller : Yes. This is Jerry Seinfeld, marketing manager at Pretty Printers. Could I speak with the Vice President of Sales?
Receiver : Alright, let me put you through.
Caller : Thanks.

* * *

Receiver : I'm sorry, the extension is busy. Would you like to hold?
Caller : Yes, please.
Receiver : Okay, I'll put you on hold.

接電話者：Huey Packford 公司。我可以為您服務嗎？
打電話者：是的，我叫傑利‧山菲爾德，普瑞迪印表機公司的行銷經理。我可以和業務部門副總裁談話嗎？
接電話者：好的，讓我為您轉接。
打電話者：謝謝。

* * *

接電話者：對不起，分機忙線中。您要等待嗎？
打電話者：是的，麻煩您。
接電話者：好的，我會將您留在線上。

4.2 某人無法接電話 Someone Is Not Available

BIZ必通句型

❶ **...IS NOT... (PLACE) TODAY.**
……今天不在……（地方）。

例 John is not here today.
約翰今天不在這兒。

例 Margaret is not in the office today.
瑪格莉特今天不在辦公室。

❷ ...IS NOT... (PLACE) AT THE MOMENT.
……現在不在……（地方）。

例 Ms. Sampson is not in her office at the moment.
辛普森女士現在不在她的辦公室。

❸ ...IS OUT TODAY.
……今天外出。

例 Stanley is out today.
史丹利今天外出。

❹ ...IS NOT AVAILABLE.
……沒有空。

例 Jordan is not available right now.
喬登現在沒空。

❺ ...IS TIED UP.
……在忙。

例 Kendra is tied up at this moment.
肯佐此刻正在忙。

當某人沒空講電話的時候，打電話的人以及接電話的人有幾個選擇，選擇如下：

• 要求留言
• 詢問是否留言

- 要求對方回電
- 表明會再回電
- 告知某人什麼時候有空

4.2a 要求留言 Leaving a Message

BIZ 必通句型

❶ CAN I LEAVE A MESSAGE (FOR...)?
我可以留言（給……）嗎？
例 Can I leave a message for Mr. Stroud?
我可以留言給史擢德先生嗎？

❷ IS IT ALRIGHT IF I LEAVE A MESSAGE (FOR...)?
我方不方便留言（給……）？
例 Is it alright if I leave a message for Mrs. Caldwell?
我方不方便留言給克威爾太太？

❸ COULD YOU TAKE A MESSAGE (FOR...)?
您可否幫我留言（給……）？
例 Could you take a message for Kate?
您可以幫我留言給凱特嗎？

❹ I'D LIKE TO LEAVE A MESSAGE IF IT'S ALRIGHT.
如果可以的話，我想要留言。

4.2b 詢問是否留言 Taking a Message

BIZ必通句型

❶ MAY I TAKE A MESSAGE?
您要留言嗎？

❷ CAN I TAKE A MESSAGE FOR YOU?
我可以幫您留言嗎？

❸ WOULD YOU LIKE TO LEAVE A MESSAGE?
您要不要留言？

❹ YOU CAN LEAVE A MESSAGE IF YOU'D LIKE.
您如果要的話，可以留言。

❺ I'D BE GLAD TO TAKE A MESSAGE.
我很樂意幫您留言。

4.2c 要求對方回電 Asking for a Return Call

BIZ必通句型

❶ COULD YOU ASK...TO GIVE ME A CALL?
您可以請……打電話給我嗎？
例 Could you ask Candice to give me a call?
您可以請甘蒂斯打電話給我嗎？

❷ COULD YOU ASK...TO CALL ME BACK?
您可以請……回電給我嗎？

例 Could you ask Mr. Brown to call me back?
您可以請布朗先生回電給我嗎?

❸ **COULD YOU ASK...TO RETURN MY CALL?**
您可以請……回我的電話嗎?
例 Could you ask Rex to return my call?
您可以請瑞克斯回我的電話嗎?

4.2d 表明會再回電 Calling Back

BIZ必通句型

❶ **I'LL CALL (...) BACK.**
我會回電(給……)。
例 I'll call her back this afternoon.
我今天下午會回電給她。

❷ **I'LL CALL (...) AGAIN.**
我會再打(給……)。
例 I'll call him again tomorrow.
我明天會再打電話給他。

❸ **I'LL CALL ANOTHER TIME.**
我改天會再打。

4.2e 告知某人什麼時候有空　Saying When Someone Is Available

BIZ 必通句型

❶ ...SHOULD BE FREE/AVAILABLE + time.

……應該在……〔時間〕有空。

例 Mr. Campbell should be free after 1:00.

堪貝爾先生應該在一點鐘之後有空。

例 Sandra should be available tomorrow.

珊卓拉明天應該有空。

❷ ...WON'T BE FREE/AVAILABLE UNTIL + time.

……要到……〔時間〕才會有空。

例 Jesse won't be free until tomorrow.

傑西要到明天才會有空。

例 Miss Sanders won't be available until 10:00.

珊德斯小姐要到十點鐘才會有空。

❸ ...CAN TAKE YOUR CALL + time.

……〔時間〕可以接你的電話。

例 Phillip can take your call this afternoon.

菲力普今天下午可以接你的電話。

❹ time + IS A GOOD TIME TO CALL BACK.

……〔時間〕是個回電的好時機。

例 Tomorrow morning is a good time to call back.

明天早上是個回電的好時機。

◇◇◇ 小心陷阱 ◇◇◇

☹ 錯誤用法

Sammi **should to be** free after lunch.

珊米午餐後應該有空。

☺ 正確用法

Sammi **should be** free after lunch.

珊米午餐後應該有空。

Show Time

❶ Receiver : Good afternoon. Calm Coffee Company.

Caller　　: Hi. May I speak to Henry Harrison, please?

Receiver : I'm sorry. Henry is out today.

Caller　　: May I leave a message for him?

Receiver : Sure.

Caller　　: I work for Pidgeon Promotions, and I would like to ask a few questions about the promotion package we put together for your company. Could you ask Henry to give me a call?

Receiver : No problem. What is your number?

接電話者：午安，寧靜咖啡公司。

打電話者：嗨，我可以和亨利·哈利森談話嗎？

接電話者：對不起，亨利今天外出。

打電話者：我可以留言給他嗎？

接電話者：當然可以。

打電話者：我在 Pidgeon 宣傳公司工作，我想要請問他幾個有關我們為貴公司舉辦的促銷活動的問題。您可以請亨利回電給我嗎？

接電話者：沒問題，請問您的電話號碼是多少？

❷ Receiver : Hello. Hualien Stone Company. Can I help you?

Caller : Hi. This is Marilyn Coleman. Is Mickey Rourke there?

Receiver : He is not in his office at the moment, but he should be available in an hour. Would you like to leave a message?

Caller : Yes, I would. I need to order some marble, and it is rather urgent.

Receiver : Okay, Ms. Coleman, I'll give him the message. Would you like Mickey to call you back?

Caller : No, that's alright. I'll call back later.

接電話者：哈囉，花蓮石業公司，我可以為您服務嗎？

打電話者：您好，我是瑪莉琳‧柯曼。請問米奇‧羅克在嗎？

接電話者：他現在不在辦公室，不過一個小時之後應該會在。您要不要留言？

打電話者：要，我要。我需要訂幾塊大理石，這件事很緊急。

接電話者：好的，柯曼女士，我會把留言交給他。要不要米奇回電給您？

打電話者：不，沒有關係。我待會再打。

4.3 狀況的釐清 Clarifying

有幾種狀況需要加以釐清。這些情況包括：
- 意思不清楚
- 說話不清楚
- 線路不清楚

4.3a 意思不清楚 Unclear Meaning

BIZ 必通句型

❶ **I'M NOT QUITE SURE WHAT YOU MEAN.**
我不太確定您的意思。

❷ **CAN YOU CLARIFY THAT?**
您可以說清楚一些嗎？

❸ **CAN YOU EXPLAIN THAT AGAIN?**
您可以再解釋一次嗎？

❹ **I'M NOT VERY CLEAR.**
我不太清楚。

❺ **CAN YOU RUN THAT BY ME AGAIN?**
您可以再向我說明一次嗎？

4.3b 說話不清楚 Unclear Speaking

BIZ 必通句型

❶ **COULD YOU SPEAK A LITTLE MORE SLOWLY?**
您可以說慢一點嗎？

COULD YOU SAY THAT AGAIN?
可以再說一遍嗎？

❸ COULD YOU SPEAK A LITTLE LOUDER?

您可以說大聲一點嗎？

❹ COULD YOU SPEAK UP A LITTLE?

您可以大聲一點說嗎？

❺ HOW DO YOU SPELL THAT?

那個字要怎麼拼？

❻ CAN YOU SPELL THAT FOR ME?

您可以幫我拼那個字嗎？

◇◇ 小心陷阱 ◇◇

☹ 錯誤用法

How **spell** that?

How **spelling**?

那個字要怎麼拼？

☺ 正確用法

How **do you spell** that?

那個字要怎麼拼？

Show Time

❶ Caller : ... So, if the shipment can't arrive by next Thursday, there will be a problem.

Receiver : Can you clarify that?

Caller : Well, I mean that I will have to cancel the order if you cannot make the Thursday delivery.

Receiver : I see.

打電話者：……那，如果無法下個禮拜四之前交貨，就會有問題。
接電話者：您可否說清楚一些？
打電話者：嗯，我的意思是說，如果你們無法於週四交貨，我就必須取消訂單。
接電話者：我懂了。

❷ Caller　　: ... The name on the invoice should be Joyce Schbley.
Receiver : How do you spell that?
Caller　　: S-c-h-b-l-e-y.
Receiver : I got it. Thanks.

打電話者：……收據上的名字應該是喬伊斯‧雪伯利。
接電話者：那個姓怎麼拼？
打電話者：S-c-h-b-l-e-y。
接電話者：我知道了，謝謝。

5 打電話的範例
Complete Example Phone Calls

本單元以下的部分，將會介紹各位一些實際的電話範例，讓各位了解如何運用本章所介紹的用語。大聲複頌這些範例，有助於加強你的記憶。

5.1 致電安排會議 Calling to Set Up a Meeting

Show Time

Edith   : Hello. This is Edith Chang of Plentiful
(Caller)   Peripherals.
Receiver : Hello. ABC Computers.
Edith   : May I speak to Gerhard Botha, please?
Receiver : May I ask what your call is regarding?
Edith   : Yes. I am calling to set up a negotiation next
            week.
Receiver : Alright, please hold.
Edith   : Thank you.

           *   *   *

Gerhard : This is Gerhard Botha.
Edith   : Mr. Botha, this is Edith Chang of Plentiful
            Peripherals.
Gerhard : Yes, hi, Edith. Nice to hear from you.
Edith   : Thanks. It's been a while since we talked. I
            hope your new product launch is going well.
Gerhard : Oh, yes, it is going very well, thanks.

Word list

peripheral〔pəˋrɪfərəl〕n. 週邊設備　　negotiation〔nɪ͵goʃɪˋeʃən〕n. 談判

Edith : I'm glad to hear that. Well, I received your letter with a suggested agenda for our negotiation. I have talked about the agenda with my team, and we would like to set up a negotiation meeting with you for next week, if possible.

Gerhard : Let me check my calendar. What day did you have in mind?

Edith : Thursday, in the afternoon if possible.

Gerhard : Let's see. ... I think Thursday afternoon of next week will work out okay. How about 2 p.m.?

Edith : 2 p.m. will work just fine for us.

Gerhard : Very good.

Edith : Okay. Let me summarize the information, then. Our negotiation will be next week, Thursday, at 2 p.m. And, as stated in your letter, the negotiation will be held at your company headquarters.

Gerhard : Yes, that's all correct.

Edith : Good. Well, I guess that's all for now, then. I appreciate you taking the time to talk with me.

Gerhard : My pleasure. See you next week.

Edith : See you. Goodbye!

Gerhard : Goodbye.

艾迪絲 ：哈囉，我是豐富電腦週邊設備公司的艾迪絲‧張。
（打電話者）

接電話者：哈囉。ABC 電腦公司。

艾迪絲 ：我可以和賈荷‧鮑撒談話嗎？

Word list

agenda〔ə`dʒɛndə〕 n. 議程　　　　headquarters〔`hɛd`kwɔrtəz〕 n. 總部

接電話者：可否請問您打電話來是要談哪方面的事情？

艾迪絲　：是的。我打電話來是要安排下個禮拜的談判會議。

接電話者：好的，請等一下。

艾迪絲　：謝謝您。

＊　　　＊　　　＊

賈荷　　：我是賈荷‧鮑撒。

艾迪絲　：鮑撒先生，我是豐富電腦週邊設備公司的艾迪絲‧張。

賈荷　　：是的，嗨，艾迪絲。很高興接到您的電話。

艾迪絲　：謝謝。自從上次我們談過之後，已經過了一段時間。我希望你們新產品的推出進行得順利。

賈荷　　：喔，是的。一切都進行得很順利，謝謝。

艾迪絲　：我很高興聽到一切順利。喔，我接到您的來信，您提出了我們談判會議的議程。我已經和我的團隊談過這個議程，如果可能的話，我們想和您約下個禮拜進行談判會議。

賈荷　　：讓我看看我的行事曆。您想要約哪一天？

艾迪絲　：如果可以的話，周四下午。

賈荷　　：讓我看看……我想下周四下午應該可以，下午兩點如何？

艾迪絲　：下午兩點可以。

賈荷　　：非常好。

艾迪絲　：好的，讓我概略重述一遍。我們的談判會議會在下個禮拜四下午兩點舉行。誠如您信中所說，談判地點將會在貴公司總部舉行。

賈荷　　：是的，正確無誤。

艾迪絲　：好的。那，我想目前就這樣了，我很感激您撥空和我談話。

賈荷　　：我的榮幸。下個禮拜見。

艾迪絲　：再見。

賈荷　　：再見。

5.2 致電索取目錄 Calling to Request a Catalog

Show Time

Joseph : Good morning. This is Joseph Lin calling from
(Caller) Kaohsiung Scooter.

Receiver : Hi, Joseph. How can I help you?

Joseph : I am calling to see if I can receive a copy of your catalog.

Receiver : I can help you with that. Are you interested in our manual tools or our electric tools?

Joseph : Both, actually. Do you have separate catalogs for the two kinds of tools?

Receiver : Yes, we do.

Joseph : Could I get one copy of each catalog?

Receiver : Sure. Let me take down your address.

Joseph : Alright. You can address it to me, Joseph Lin, 1001 Ren Ai Road, Section 15, Taipei 101, Taiwan.

Receiver : Let me repeat that, okay?

Joseph : Sure.

Receiver : Joseph Lin. 1001 Ren Ai Road, Section 15. Taipei 101. Taiwan.

Joseph : That's correct.

Receiver : I'll put the two catalogs in the mail this afternoon.

Joseph : Thank you very much.

Receiver : You're welcome.

Joseph : Bye bye.

Receiver : Goodbye.

喬瑟夫　　：早安。我是高雄摩托車公司的喬瑟夫‧林。
（打電話者）

接電話者：嗨，喬瑟夫。我可以為您效勞嗎？

喬瑟夫　　：我打電話來想問貴公司是否可以寄一份目錄給我。

接電話者：這我可以幫您。請問您對我們的手動工具、還是電動工具有興趣？

喬瑟夫　　：兩種都有。這兩種工具的目錄是分開的嗎？

接電話者：是的。

喬瑟夫　　：我可以這兩種各拿一份嗎？

接電話者：當然可以。讓我記下您的地址。

喬瑟夫　　：好的。您可以寄到台灣，台北，郵遞區號101，仁愛路十五段，1001號，喬瑟夫‧林收。

接電話者：讓我重複一遍，好嗎？

喬瑟夫　　：當然。

接電話者：喬瑟夫‧林。台灣，台北，郵遞區號101，仁愛路十五段，1001號。

喬瑟夫　　：對。

接電話者：我今天下午會把這兩份目錄郵寄給您。

喬瑟夫　　：非常謝謝您。

接電話者：不客氣。

喬瑟夫　　：再見。

接電話者：再見。

5.3 接獲下訂單的電話 Receiving a Call to Place an Order

Show Time

Receiver : Good afternoon.　Taichung Tectronics.

Dana　　 : Good afternoon.　I am Dana Andrews, a

Purchaser at Auto Teddy in the United States. Is one of your salespeople available?

Receiver : Yes. Please hold on a moment while I transfer you.

Dana : Thank you.

*　　　*　　　*

Michael : Hello. This is Michael Hu. May I help you?

Dana : Hi, Michael. This is Dana Andrews with Auto Teddy in the United States.

Michael : Hi, Dana. I'm afraid your regular salesperson, Amanda, isn't here today. But I will try to help you.

Dana : Thanks. I'm sure you can help me. By the way, I heard the weather there is very hot recently.

Michael : Yes, very hot. But it must be hot where you live, too.

Dana : It is hot, but not so humid like Taiwan.

Michael : I see.

Dana : Well, the reason I am calling is to order 4,000 chips for the new version of our talking teddy bear.

Michael : Okay. Have you made any prior arrangements for this with Amanda?

Dana : I talked to her last week, and she said the chips would be available for shipment any time this week. She said your company would have up to 6,000 available.

Michael : Yes, I think we have about 6,000 in stock, so

we can certainly supply you with 4,000.

Dana : And the standard 5% discount applies, right?

Michael : Yes. Any order above 2,000 receives a 5% discount.

Dana : Okay. Then, if you can begin to package the chips for shipment, I will prepare to send a wire transfer. The only other thing is that I want to confirm the shipment date.

Michael : We can package the chips today, and they will be ready for shipment tomorrow. We will ship them the same day we receive the wire.

Dana : Good. I will prepare the wire and call you as soon as it is sent. I would like to go over the details of everything if you don't mind.

Michael : Certainly.

Dana : I am ordering 4,000 chips for our talking teddy bear. The chips sell for 2 U.S. dollars a piece. So that is 8,000 U.S. dollars. There is a 5% discount, which comes to 400 dollars. So, the total amount is 7,600 U.S. dollars.

Michael : That is all correct.

Dana : Everything seems to be in order. I will call you soon to let you know about the wire. Thanks for your help.

Michael : You're welcome!

Dana : Goodbye.

Michael : Bye.

接電話者：午安，台中電子技術公司。

戴納	：午安。我是戴納‧安德魯斯，美國自動泰迪熊公司的採購人員。請問貴公司的業務人員有空嗎？
接電話者	：有的。請等一下，我幫您轉接過去。
戴納	：謝謝您。

*   *   *

麥可	：哈囉，我是麥可‧胡。可以為您服務嗎？
戴納	：嗨，麥可。我是美國自動泰迪熊公司的戴納‧安德魯斯。
麥可	：嗨，戴納。您平常的業務人員阿曼達今天不在這兒。不過我可以設法幫您。
戴納	：謝謝。我確定你可以幫我。對了，聽說你們那邊最近天氣很熱。
麥可	：是的，非常熱。不過你住的地方一定也很熱。
戴納	：的確很熱，不過沒有像台灣那麼潮濕。
麥可	：這樣子呀。
戴納	：嗯，我打電話的目的是要為我們新款會講話的泰迪熊訂購四千個晶片。
麥可	：好的。先前阿曼達有對此幫您作過任何安排嗎？
戴納	：我上個禮拜和她談過，她說這些晶片這個禮拜隨時可以出貨。她說貴公司庫存有六千個。
麥可	：是的，我想我們庫存大約有六千個，所以我們一定可以提供你們四千個。
戴納	：那麼百分之五的標準折扣依然適用，對不對？
麥可	：是的，只要是超過兩千個的訂單，都可以獲得百分之五的折扣。
戴納	：好的，如果你們可以開始打包這些晶片準備出貨，我就可以準備把錢匯過去。另外我唯一要確認的是出貨日期。
麥可	：我們今天可以打包這些晶片，以便明天準備運送。在我

們收到匯款的同一天就會出貨。

戴納 ：好的。我會準備好匯款，一匯過去我就會打電話通知您。如果您不介意的話，我想要再重複一次細節。

麥可 ：當然沒有問題。

戴納 ：我為我們會講話的泰迪熊訂購了四千個晶片。這些晶片單價為二美元，總共應為八千美元。百分之五的折扣為四百美元，因此總價為七千六百美元。

麥可 ：全部正確。

戴納 ：一切似乎都沒問題了。我會很快打電話過來，讓您知道匯款的情況。謝謝您的協助。

麥可 ：不客氣！

戴納 ：再見。

麥可 ：再見

Remember the Principles

1 你們不用背下所有意思相同的片語或是句子。只要從每個主題當中選出一個片語或是句子的範例記下來即可。讓它成為你天然的風格。

You do not need to memorize all phrases or sentences that have the same meaning. Pick one phrase or sentence example from each topic area and memorize it. Let that become your natural style.

2 確定電話的關鍵資訊夠清楚。提供、接收或交換資訊都是講電話的目的。

Make sure the key information of your phone calls is clear. Giving, receiving, or exchanging information are the purposes of phone calls.

6 實戰演練　Partner Practice

根據下列情境，找個同伴一起模擬對話，作爲實戰前的演練。

❶ A是台灣人，B是在自己國家的西方人。

A打電話給B，訂購某種產品（自己決定是哪種產品——比如某項你們公司需要向海外訂購的產品）。

A：自我介紹，要求和B談話

B：回答

A：說明打電話的目的

B：打開對話

A：簡短的對話

B：簡短的對話

A：詳細說明要求

B：摘要對方要求

A：總結

B：總結

A：說再見

B：說再見

第 5 章

作簡報
Presentation

　　作簡報令許多人緊張不已，有人說只有看牙醫是比作簡報更可怕的事！不過，你可以培養這方面的信心，也可以發表出色的簡報。就如同其他形式的正式溝通，作簡報也是有步驟可以遵循的。只要了解這些步驟以及每一步所需的英文用語即可。本章將提供你所需要的基本口語技巧。

　　Giving a presentation makes many people nervous. Some say only going to the dentist is worse than giving a presentation! However, you can develop confidence and deliver very good presentations. As with all other forms of formal communication, there is a process for presentations. Just understand this process and the English needed for each part of the process. This chapter gives you the basic oral skills that you need.

1 簡報的說明 Talking about Presentations

　　簡報是利用視覺輔助器材所做的演講。本章節的重點放在作專業簡報時所需用到的語彙。雖然運用視覺輔助器材有其重要性，而且需要相關的知識和技巧，不過視覺輔助器材的使用方法並不包含在本章節的範圍內。

　　要學習成功地作簡報，必須先具備一些基本字彙。這些基本字彙在作簡報時會很有幫助，而且也有助於各位談論有關作簡報的事項。

1.1 基本的字彙 Basic Vocabulary

　　請記住以下字彙。

BIZ必通字彙

正式口語溝通類型 (Kinds of Formal Oral Communication)
❶ talk〔tɔk〕*n.* 演說　　　　❷ speech〔spitʃ〕*n.* 演講
❸ lecture〔`lɛktʃə〕*n.* 講演
❹ presentation〔͵prɛzn̩`teʃən〕*n.* 簡報

參與者 (People)
❶ presenter〔prɪ`zɛntə〕*n.* 報告人
❷ speaker〔`spikə〕*n.* 演講者　❸ lecturer〔`lɛktʃərə〕*n.* 演講者
❹ audience〔`ɔdɪəns〕*n.* 聽眾

視覺輔助材料種類 (Types of Visual Aids)
❶ overhead〔͵ovə`hɛd〕*n.* 投影片
❷ video〔`vɪdɪ͵o〕*n.* 錄影帶　❸ handout〔`hændaut〕*n.* 講義
❹ realia〔rɪ`ælɪə〕*n.* 實物

視覺輔助器材 (Equipment for Visual Aids)
❶ overhead projector〔ˌovɚˋhɛd prəˋdʒɛktɚ〕*n.* 投影機
❷ video player〔ˋvɪdɪˌo ˋpleɚ〕*n.* 放影機
❸ whiteboard〔ˋhwaɪtˌbord〕*n.* 白板
❹ flip chart〔ˋflɪp ˌtʃɑrt〕*n.*（可翻閱的）圖表架

1.2 配合情境的字彙 Vocabulary in Context

　　在電話的章節裡提過，學習單字時配合例句的上下文是很重要的，這樣才能完全了解如何使用這些字彙。在下列 1.2 的部分，會看到前面提過的所有字彙以及這些字彙的例句。注意這些字的用法，這樣才能靈活運用到其他句子裡。

　　小叮嚀：把例句大聲朗讀出來，每個句子至少一遍，如此反覆朗讀是學習使用字彙的好方法。練習的次數愈多，這些句型就愈能深刻烙印在腦海之中。要流利地使用一個語言，最基本的要求就是靈活運用各種句型，並且在需要的句型當中代換不同的字彙。

1.2a 「正式口語溝通類型」的字彙
'Kinds of Formal Oral Communication' Vocabulary

Show Time

❶ I am glad you could attend my **talk**.　I just want to share a few observations about my trip to the Middle East.
很高興你們能參加入我的演說，我只是想分享一些中東之行的觀察心得。

Word list

the Middle East〔ðə ˋmɪdl̩ ist〕*n.* 中東

❷ In my **speech** today I will explain three reasons why we need to revise our five-year plan.
在今天的演講裡，我將解釋為什麼我們的五年計畫需要修正的三項理由。

❸ In today's **lecture** I will explain one method for analyzing theories of economics.
在今天的講演裡，我將說明一個分析經濟理論的方法。

❹ In this **presentation** I will show you how to operate the new version of our DVD player.
我會在此次簡報中向各位展示新版 DVD 放映機的操作方法。

1.2b 「參與者」的字彙 'People' Vocabulary

Show Time

❶ Today's **presenter** is Alvin McCoy, the manager of our accounting department.
今天作簡報的人是我們會計部門經理，艾文‧麥考伊。

❷ Our **speaker** this afternoon will introduce our new marketing plan.
我們今天下午的主講人將會介紹我們新的行銷計畫。

❸ Our **lecturer** is Bob Jones, Professor of Business at Kansas Institute of Technology.
我們的主講人是鮑伯‧瓊斯，堪薩斯理工學院的商學教授。

❹ You have been a wonderful **audience**. Thanks for your attention!
各位是很棒的聽眾。謝謝各位的聆聽！

◇◇◇ 小心陷阱 ◇◇◇

☹ 錯誤用法
Our **lecture** today is Missy Clapton.
我們今天的主講人是蜜西‧克萊普頓。

☺ 正確用法
Our **lecturer** today is Missy Clapton.
我們今天的主講人是蜜西‧克萊普頓。

1.2c 「視覺輔助材料種類」的字彙 'Types of Visual Aids' Vocabulary

Show Time

❶ I will be using some **overheads** to show you different views of our new factory in China.
我會利用一些投影片向各位展現我們在中國新廠房的不同風貌。

❷ Tonight I will show you some **video** clips of proper ways to use the new equipment.
我今晚會放一些錄影片段，示範如何正確使用新的裝備。

❸ Everybody please take one **handout**. The handout presents the specifications of the NCC1701 model airplane.

Word list

institute〔`ɪnstətjut〕*n.* 學院　　specification〔ˌspɛsəfə`keʃən〕*n.* 規格；設計書

請每個人都拿一份講義。這份資料說明了 NCC1701 模型飛機的規格。

❹ I have brought some **realia** with me so that you can actually see and touch the new watch design.
我帶了一些實物過來,這樣你們就可以實際看到並觸摸這個新款手錶。

1.2d 「視覺輔助器材」的字彙 'Equipment for Visual Aids' Vocabulary

Show Time

❶ Please turn off the lights so we can use the **overhead projector**.
請把燈關掉,我們好使用投影機。

❷ We need a **video player** to play the video clips this morning.
今天上午我們需要一台放映機播放幾段影片。

❸ I will write the important points on the **whiteboard**.
我會把重點寫在白板上。

❹ As I give my presentation, I will use this **flip chart** to show you the main idea of each section.
我會在報告時使用這個圖表架,向各位說明每個部分的主旨。

2 簡報的基本要素　Basic Parts of a Presentation

　　各位得熟悉簡報幾個基本要素當中的英文用語。以下四個項目是所有的簡報都會包含的部分。

　　基本項目：

1. 簡介
2. 主體
3. 總結
4. 提問與回答

　　這幾個部分會用到的英文在接下來的章節（2.1～2.4）中會加以解釋。讀例句時，請注意句型以及用法。

　　小叮嚀：將所學的英文運用到真實生活中的最好方法就是從每個段落選取一兩個例句，然後將這些例句熟記起來。一而再、再而三地反覆練習，直到能脫口而出為止。挑選的例句最好能配合你的個性、風格，或是與你的工作情境有所關聯。

2.1 簡介　Introductions

　　簡報開場的介紹可分為幾個部分：

- 問候
- 自我介紹
- 主題／題目／目的
- 簡報的長度
- 事先的概要說明
- 問答

　　以上這些項目在簡報中的順序並不是固定的。上面所排列的順序是最普遍的排法，你也可以依照自己的方式做一些調整。

2.1a 問候 Greeting

BIZ必通句型

❶ GOOD MORNING/AFTERNOON/EVENING.
早安 / 午安 / 晚安。

❷ WELCOME TO...
歡迎來到……
例 Welcome to our company headquarters. I am glad to see all of you.
歡迎蒞臨本公司總部。我很高興見到各位。

❸ IT IS AN HONOR TO...
很榮幸……
例 It is an honor to be able to present our new product to our special visitors from overseas.
很榮幸能夠為我們來自海外的貴賓們介紹本公司的新產品。

❹ IT IS A PLEASURE TO...
很高興……
例 It is a pleasure to be here in your Los Angeles Office tonight.
很高興今晚來到貴公司的洛杉磯辦事處。

❺ I AM HAPPY TO...
我很高興……
例 I am happy to be here today so that I can tell you some exciting news.
我很高興今天來到這裡，告訴你們一些令人興奮的消息。

例 I am happy to be able to tell you about our industrial plan.

我很高興能夠告訴各位我們的產業計畫。

❻ I AM PLEASED TO HAVE THIS OPPORTUNITY TO...

我很高興有這個機會……

例 I am pleased to have this opportunity to address this wonderful audience.

我很高興有這個機會向各位這群很棒的聽眾發表演說。

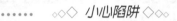

◇◇◇ 小心陷阱 ◇◇◇

☹ 錯誤用法

I am **please** to have this opportunity to talk to you.

我很高興有這個機會能夠與你談話。

☺ 正確用法

I am **pleased** to have this opportunity to talk to you.

我很高興有這個機會能夠與你談話。

2.1b 自我介紹 Self-introduction

自我介紹當中應該包含姓名、公司以及職稱。至於很明顯的訊息就不需要多作說明，否則就嫌多餘了。可以參考第一章中的方法來自我介紹，因為不論你的對象是一群聽眾還是單獨一人，自我介紹的方式基本上是一樣的。下列的範例是特別針對簡報時的自我介紹。

BIZ必通句型

❶ I WOULD LIKE TO BEGIN BY TELLING YOU A BIT ABOUT MYSELF.
首先我想向各位自我介紹一下。

❷ ALLOW ME TO TELL YOU A BIT ABOUT MYSELF.
請容我向各位簡單地自我介紹。

❸ I WOULD LIKE TO BEGIN BY TELLING YOU A LITTLE ABOUT MY BACKGROUND.
我想要先向各位稍微介紹一下我的背景。

❹ ALLOW ME TO BEGIN BY TELLING YOU A LITTLE ABOUT MY BACKGROUND.
首先請容我向各位稍微介紹一下我的背景。

❺ I WOULD LIKE TO TAKE THIS OPPORTUNITY TO INTRODUCE MYSELF.
我想藉這個機會自我介紹一下。

❻ ALLOW ME TO TAKE THIS OPPORTUNITY TO INTRODUCE MYSELF.
容我藉這個機會自我介紹一下。

❼ LET ME INTRODUCE MYSELF, I AM...
讓我自我介紹一下，我是……
例 Let me introduce myself, I am Alfred Himler, a specialist in management systems.
讓我自我介紹一下。我是愛佛瑞德‧漢姆勒，管理系統的專家。

◇◇◇ 小心陷阱 ◇◇◇

☹ 錯誤用法

I **like** to begin by telling you a bit about myself.

首先我想向各位簡單地自我介紹。

☺ 正確用法

I **would like** to begin by telling you a bit about myself.

首先我想向各位簡單地自我介紹。

2.1c 主題／題目／目的 Topic/Title/Purpose

BIZ必通句型

❶ THE TOPIC/TITLE/PURPOSE OF MY PRESENTATION IS...

我簡報的主題／題目／目的是……

例 The topic of my presentation is about joint ventures with Italian companies.

我簡報的主題是有關與義大利企業的聯合投資。

例 The title of my presentation is "Joint Ventures with Italian Companies."

我簡報的題目是「與義大利企業的聯合投資」。

例 The purpose of my presentation is to help you understand how to have a successful joint venture with an Italian company.

我簡報的目的在於協助各位了解如何成功地與義大利企業聯合投資。

Word list

joint venture〔ˋdʒɔɪnt ˋvɛntʃɚ〕n. 合資經營

❷ I WANT TO TALK TO YOU ABOUT...

我想跟各位談談……

例 I want to talk to you about the new tax-free development zone.

我想跟各位談談新的免稅開發區。

❸ I AM GOING TO PRESENT...

我將要提出……

例 I am going to present the latest sales figures.

我將向各位提出最新的銷售數字。

❹ I AM HERE TODAY TO...

我今天在這裡是為了……

例 I am here today to give you a presentation about our direct sales techniques.

我今天來這裡是要向各位介紹我們的直銷技巧。

❺ WHAT I AM GOING TO TALK ABOUT IS...

我將要談的是……

例 What I am going to talk about is the emerging industrial parks in Vietnam.

我將要談的是，越南的新興工業園區。

Word list

figure〔`fɪgjɚ〕n. 數字

◇◇◇ 小心陷阱 ◇◇◇

☹ 錯誤用法

I am going to talk about is my new project.

我將要談的是我的新專案。

☺ 正確用法

What I am going to talk about is my new project.

我將要談的是我的新專案。

2.1d 簡報的長度 Length

　　一般來說，西方人都很注重時間，這一點請特別注意。因此他們會想知道報告的時間有多長，這樣才好有心理準備，同時，也可以掌握時間，以便在報告結束後進行接下來的活動。

BIZ必通句型

❶ **MY PRESENTATION WILL TAKE (ABOUT)＋time**

我報告的時間約為……

例 My presentation will take about ten minutes.

我報告的時間約為十分鐘。

❷ **I WILL TAKE (ABOUT)＋time**

我將花（大約）……

例 I will take thirty minutes.

我將花三十分鐘的時間。

❸ **I WILL ONLY TAKE...MINUTES OF YOUR TIME.**

我只會占用各位……分的時間。

例 I will only take twenty minutes of your time.

我只會占用各位二十分鐘的時間。

❹ THE PRESENTATION SHOULD LAST (ABOUT)＋ time

簡報將進行（大約）……

例 The presentation should last fifteen minutes.

簡報將進行十五分鐘。

例 The presentation should last only about five minutes.

簡報大約只須五分鐘。

❺ MY PRESENTATION WILL END AT ＋ time

我的簡報將於……結束。

例 My presentation will end at 4:30.

我的簡報將於4:30結束。

◇◇◇ 小心陷阱 ◇◇◇

☹ 錯誤用法

The presentation **should taking** about one hour.

簡報將須大約一個鐘頭的時間。

☺ 正確用法

The presentation **should take** about one hour.

簡報將須大約一個鐘頭的時間。

2.1e 事先的概要說明 Preview

　　西方人簡報的形式偏重在協助聽眾記住報告的重點或主旨。簡報過程中會提到這些重點或主旨三次，分別是：簡介、主體內容、結論。報告人會在簡介階段先行預告重點，然後才在報告主體當中詳細解釋。最後，到了結論時，再為這些重點作個總結。

BIZ必通句型

說明簡報分為幾個部分的說法：

❶ **MY PRESENTATION HAS...PARTS.**
我的簡報分為……個部分。
> 例 My presentation has three parts.
> 我的報告分為三個部分。

❷ **I HAVE DIVIDED MY PRESENTATION INTO...**
我把我的簡報分為……
> 例 I have divided my presentation into four parts.
> 我把我的簡報分為四個部分。
> 例 I have divided my presentation into two sections.
> 我把我的簡報分為兩大部分。
> 例 I have divided my presentation into three areas.
> 我把我的簡報分成三個領域。

❸ **I'LL BE COVERING...**
我將會討論到……
> 例 I will be covering four ideas.
> 我將會討論到四個構想。
> 例 I will be covering three myths.
> 我將會討論到三個迷思。
> 例 I will be covering five potential markets.
> 我將會討論到五個潛在市場。

Word list

potential market〔pə`tɛnʃəl `mɑrkɪt〕*n.* 潛在市場

❹ MY PRESENTATION WILL COVER...

我將在簡報中討論……

例 My presentation will cover three new ideas.

我將在簡報中討論三個新構想。

◇◇◇ 小心陷阱 ◇◇◇

☹ 錯誤用法

I **divide** my presentation into three parts.

我把我的簡報分成三個部分。

☺ 正確用法

I **have divided** my presentation into three parts.

我把我的簡報分成三個部分

BIZ 必通句型

說明簡報各部分的說法：

❶ FIRST... SECOND... THIRD...

第一點……第二點……第三點……

例 First, the price. Second, the target market. Third, the sales projection.

第一點，價錢。第二點，目標市場。第三點，業績預估。

❷ THE FIRST...IS... THE SECOND...IS...

第一……為……第二……為……

Word list

target market〔`tɑrgɪt `mɑrkɪt〕*n.* 目標市場

sales projection〔`selz prə`dʒɛkʃən〕*n.* 業績預測

例 The first part is the price. The second part is the target market. The third part is the sales projection.

第一個部分為價錢。第二個部分為目標市場。第三部分為業績預估。

❸ **FIRST I'D LIKE TO... SECOND I'D LIKE TO... FINALLY I'D LIKE TO...**

首先我要……其次我要……最後我要……

例 First I'd like to discuss the issue of fairness. Second I'd like to discuss the issue of accountability. And third I'd like to discuss the issue of leadership.

首先我要來討論公平的問題。其次我要探討責任的問題。最後我要探討領導的問題。

❹ **THE...I WILL BE...ARE...**

我要談的……是……

例 The ideas I will be presenting are quality, appeal, and perception.

我將要提出的想法是品質、吸引力以及洞察力。

例 The points I will be addressing are effectiveness, excellence, and perseverance.

我要講的重點是效率、卓越以及毅力。

❺ **THE MAIN PARTS ARE...**

主要的部分為……

Word list

accountability〔ə,kaʊntə`bɪlətɪ〕*n.* 負有責任或義務

perseverance〔,pɝsə`vɪrəns〕*n.* 毅力；不屈不撓

例 The main parts are external condition, internal condition, and reality of condition.
主要的部分為外部狀況、內部狀況，以及實際的狀況。

◇◇◇ 小心陷阱 ◇◇◇

☹ 錯誤用法
The **point** I will be discussing are debt and borrowing.
我要討論的重點是債務與借貸。
☺ 正確用法
The **points** I will be discussing are debt and borrowing.
我要討論的重點是債務與借貸。

2.1f 提問與回答 Question & Answer

　　每一個簡報都需要聽眾提出一些問題，來達到互動的效果。讓聽眾發問可以用兩種方式進行。聽眾可以在報告進行中隨時提問，或是報告結束後，留一些時間讓聽眾發問。

BIZ必通句型

隨時可發問的說法：

❶ ...PLEASE INTERRUPT (AT) ANY TIME...
……請隨時打斷……

Word list

interrupt〔͵ɪntəˋrʌpt〕v. 打斷；阻止

例 Please interrupt any time you have a question.
你們有問題請隨時提出來。

例 Please interrupt any time you want to ask me something.
如果你們想問我問題，請隨時打斷我。

例 If you have a question, please interrupt at any time.
如果你們有問題，請隨時提出來。

❷ YOU CAN INTERRUPT THE PRESENTATION AT ANY TIME.
各位可以隨時打斷報告的進行。

❸ FEEL FREE TO INTERRUPT THE PRESENTATION AT ANY TIME.
各位儘管隨時打斷報告的進行。

❹ YOU MAY INTERRUPT AT ANY TIME.
你們可以隨時打斷。

❺ YOU MAY INTERRUPT ANY TIME YOU HAVE A QUESTION.
你們一有問題，就可以隨時打斷。

BIZ必通句型

將問題保留到最後的說法：

❶ PLEASE HOLD YOUR QUESTIONS UNTIL THE END OF THE PRESENTATION.
請將你們的問題保留到報告結束再提出來。

② **PLEASE SAVE YOUR QUESTIONS UNTIL AFTER THE PRESENTATION.**

請將你的問題留到報告完後再提。

③ **IF YOU HAVE ANY QUESTIONS, I WILL ANSWER THEM WHEN I HAVE FINISHED MY PRESENTATION.**

如果各位有任何疑問，我會在報告結束後再答覆。

④ **THERE WILL BE TIME FOR QUESTIONS AT THE END OF MY PRESENTATION.**

我的簡報結束後會留一些時間讓各位發問。

⑤ **I WILL TAKE ANY QUESTIONS AT THE END OF MY PRESENTATION.**

簡報結束後我會回答各位的問題。

◇◇◇ 小心陷阱 ◇◇◇

☹ 錯誤用法

Please **saving** your questions until after the presentation.

請將你的問題留到報告結束後再提。

☺ 正確用法

Please **save** your questions until after the presentation.

請將你的問題留到報告結束後再提。

Show Time

Good morning. It is a pleasure to be with you today. Allow me to tell you a bit about myself. I am Kennedy

Oldman, an engineer at Tokyo Steel. I have worked in the steel business for fifteen years.

I want to talk to you about our steel production process. I will be covering three topics. First, our raw materials. Second, our production techniques. And Third, our storage methods.

I will only take twenty to twenty-five minutes of your time. Please save your questions until after the presentation.

早安，很高興今天見到各位。讓我先跟各位介紹一下自己。我是甘迺迪‧歐德曼，東京鋼鐵的工程師。我從事鋼鐵業已經有十五年的時間了。

我想跟各位談談我們的鋼鐵生產過程。我將會談論三個主題。首先是我們的原料。其次是我們的生產技術。第三是我們的儲存方法。

我只會耽誤各位二十至二十五分鐘的時間。請各位將問題留到報告結束後再發問。

2.2 主體　Bodies

簡報主體內容並沒有特定的英文用語。只要把握明確、直接的溝通原則即可。盡量舉例說明，讓聽眾確實了解你的意思。

雖然報告的主體本身並沒有特定的英文用語，但是報告的內容當中會用到許多連接以及轉折的詞語，這些用語將留到本章第三部分再加以解釋。

西方人的報告方式是採用推論的思考方式。一開始先闡述主要的觀點，然後再詳細解釋或舉例說明這個觀點。因此在談到每個部分的內容

之前，先闡明你的重點，條理分明地陳述，甚至可以一再重複。在本章最後的4.3節，有一些報告的範例可以更清楚地解釋這一點。

2.3 總結 Conclusions

總結可分為四個部分：
- 進行總結的開場白
- 重點的摘要說明
- 說明自己的期許
- 結語

2.3a 進行總結的開場白 Conclusion Signal

BIZ必通句型

❶ **THAT CONCLUDES THE MAIN POINTS OF MY PRESENTATION.**
我報告的重點到這裡結束。

❷ **THAT FINISHES MY PRESENTATION.**
我的報告到此結束。

❸ **I HAVE COME TO THE END OF MY PRESENTATION.**
我的報告已經接近尾聲。

❹ **THAT BRINGS ME TO THE END OF MY PRESENTATION.**
我的報告在此告一段落。

❺ WE'VE ARRIVED AT THE END OF MY PRESENTATION.

我的報告已經到了尾聲。

◇◇◇ 小心陷阱 ◇◇◇

☹ 錯誤用法

That **finish** my presentation.

我的報告到此結束。

☺ 正確用法

That **finishes** my presentation.

我的報告到此結束。

2.3b 重點的摘要說明 Summary of Main Points

BIZ必通句型

❶ ...SUMMARIZE THE MAIN POINTS/TOPICS.

……總結要點／主題。

例 Let me summarize the main points.

讓我把要點作個總結。

例 I'd like to summarize the main topics.

我想把主題作個總結。

❷ ...GO OVER THE MAIN POINTS/TOPICS AGAIN.

……再重複一遍要點／主題。

例 Let me go over the main points again.

讓我把要點再重述一遍。

例 I'd like to go over the main topics again.

我想再把主題重述一次。

❸ LET'S RECAP.
讓我們把要點重複一遍。

❹ LET'S SUMMARIZE.
我們來作個總結。

❺ LET ME OFFER YOU A QUICK SUMMARY.
讓我幫你們很快地作個總結。

2.3c 說明自己的期許 Statement of Hope

　　我們之所以進行簡報是因為有所期望。你希望這個報告能夠讓聽眾因而有所省思或是一些作為。那麼，你期待聽眾有什麼省思？你所期望的就是聽眾能認同你提出的看法；或是你提出一個新的想法，希望聽眾能夠理解。你希望聽眾有什麼樣的作為？你希望聽眾採取的行動可能有許多不同的類型。譬如，你希望聽眾購買某些東西，或是銷售某些東西。

　　你的期望就是你進行簡報的原因。而這也正是整個報告的關鍵構想。在結論中應將這些想法清晰地加以闡述。

*BIZ*必通句型

❶ I SUGGEST...
我建議……
例 I suggest that you consider the ideas I have presented. I think you will see they make sense.

Word list

recap〔`rikæp〕*v.* 重述要旨

我建議各位考慮我所提出的想法。我想你們會明白這些想法的確有道理。

例 I suggest you look closely at our product and place an order today.

我建議各位仔細看看我們的產品,並且今天就下訂單。

❷ I HOPE...

我希望……

例 I hope you will accept the three core ideas and remember them as you begin your new project.

我希望各位能接受這三個主要的概念,並且在各位展開新專案時將這些想法謹記在心。

例 I hope you have learned something about our marketing techniques so that you can be the best marketing team in our industry!

希望各位已經習得一些我們的行銷技巧,這樣你們才能成為我們這一行的最佳行銷團隊。

❸ IT IS MY HOPE THAT...

我的期望是……

例 It is my hope that you will all try these techniques in your own business.

我的期望是各位都能嘗試將這些技巧運用到自己的事業上。

❹ I ENCOURAGE YOU TO...

我鼓勵你們……

例 I encourage you to remember these four ideas so that you can do a better job selling the new line of products.

我鼓勵各位將這四個概念記牢,這樣各位在銷售這一系列新產品時會有更好的表現。

❺ I CHALLENGE YOU TO...
我請各位……
例 I challenge you to improve your management skills using the ideas I have presented here.
我激勵各位以我在此介紹的點子改善你們的管理技巧。

2.3d 結語 Close

結語就是用一句話告訴聽眾你的報告已經結束了。簡單句是最好的選擇！

*BIZ*必通句型

❶ THANK YOU!
謝謝！

❷ THANK YOU FOR...
謝謝……
例 Thank you for attending.
謝謝各位的參與。
例 Thank you for listening.
謝謝各位的聽講。
例 Thank you for coming today.
謝謝各位今天出席。

Word list

challenge〔`tʃælɪndʒ〕 v. 激勵

❸ THANK YOU FOR YOUR...

謝謝……

例 Thank you for your attention.

謝謝各位的聆聽。

例 Thank you for your attendance.

謝謝各位的出席。

例 Thank you for your time.

謝謝各位撥冗前來。

Show Time

I have come to the end of my presentation. Let's summarize. First, I told you the sources of our raw materials. Second, I explained our production techniques. And finally, I outlined our storage methods.

It is my hope that you better understand our company now, since we will be doing business together.

Thank you for listening.

我的報告已經接近尾聲。讓我來作個總結。首先,我跟各位說了我們原料的來源。第二,我解釋了我們的生產技術。最後,我概括解釋了我們的庫存方法。

我的期望是各位現在對本公司已有進一步了解,因為我們將會一起合作。

謝謝各位的聽講。

2.4 提問與答覆 Question And Answer

簡報結束後都應有一段開放性的時間，讓聽眾發問。簡報結束時，可以說一些話來提醒聽眾，讓他們知道可以發問。

BIZ必通句型

❶ I WOULD BE HAPPY TO ANSWER ANY QUESTIONS.
我很樂意回答任何問題。

❷ DOES ANYBODY HAVE A QUESTION?
有沒有人有問題？

❸ ARE THERE ANY QUESTIONS I CAN ANSWER?
有沒有什麼我可以解答的問題？

❹ NOW I WILL TAKE YOUR QUESTIONS.
現在我可以接受發問。

❺ I'LL TAKE YOUR QUESTIONS NOW.
我現在會回答各位的問題。

◇◇◇ 小心陷阱 ◇◇◇

☹ 錯誤用法
Is anybody have a question?
有沒有人有問題？
☺ 正確用法
Does anybody have a question?
有沒有人有問題？

3 連結簡報各要素的方法
Connecting Parts of a Presentation

　　點子會在腦海裡形成1、2、3、4或是A、B、C、D之類的序列。第1點和第2點有關係，第2點和第1、3點有關係。A和B有關，B則和A、C有關。所以，線性思考模式意味著 (1) 一次說明一個想法，(2) 說明每個想法的時候都要表達清楚。

　　有一種特殊的英文用語可以套用在這種線性思考模式上。這種特殊用語必須用在簡報的每個要素上：簡介、主體、以及結論。這些適用於線性思考的用語包括：

- 標示
- 連結
- 轉接

　　標示和連結的用語不多，各自有一些簡單的說法，所以容易記憶。轉接的用語則有較多的種類，不過每一種類都有一些簡單的表達方法。

3.1 標示 Tagging

　　標示用語是告訴聽眾主講人報告到什麼部分。簡報應該有許多標示之處。如果報告的時候不加以標示，那麼聽眾會不知道你在談論哪個部份，並因此而感到困惑。

*BIZ*必通句型

**❶ FIRST,... SECOND,... THIRD,... NEXT,...
LAST/FINALLY,...**

第一……第二……第三……接下來……最後……

例 First, let's talk about the cost of the new magazine.
　　首先，讓我談談這本新雜誌的成本。

例 Next, I want to discuss the recent infrastructure improvements.
接下來，我想要討論最近在基礎結構方面所做的改善。

例 Fourth, I want to explain the importance of the new budgetary procedure.
第四，我想要說明新預算程序的重要性。

❷ THE FIRST... THE SECOND... THE NEXT... THE LAST/FINAL...
第一……第二……接下來……最後……

例 The first thing I want to talk about is the product's image.
第一件我想討論的事項是這產品的形象。

例 The next issue is the negotiation between us and IBM.
接下來的議題是我們和 IBM 之間的談判。

例 The final question is whether we should expand our factory in Tainan.
最後一個問題是我們應不應該拓展在台南的工廠。

3.2 連結 Linking

連結的用語可以讓聽眾知道一個部分已經告一段落，或是一個部分即將開始。連結用語可能是個簡短的介紹或是結論。簡報應該要有許多連結語。如果不使用這些連結語，聽眾可能不知道你是否已講完一個部分，或是你要開始講另外一個部分。

ord list

infrastructure〔`ɪnfrə,strʌktʃɚ〕n. 基礎結構；基礎設施

3.2a 結束某個主題或是重點 Ending a Topic or Point

*BIZ*必通句型

❶ THAT COVERS...

以上就是……的介紹。

例 That covers my second point.

以上就是我第二個論點的介紹。

例 That covers the issue of salary raises.

以上就是有關加薪議題的說明。

❷ LET'S LEAVE...

讓我將……告一段落。

例 Let's leave the topic of promotions.

促銷的主題在此告一段落。

例 Let's leave that now.

那部份在此告一段落。

◇◇ 小心陷阱 ◇◇

☹ 錯誤用法

That's cover my first point.

以上是我第一個論點的說明。

☺ 正確用法

That covers my first point.

以上是我第一個論點的說明。

3.2b 開始某個主題或是重點 Beginning a Topic or Point

BIZ必通句型

❶ LET'S START WITH...

讓我們先從……開始。

例 Let's start with the pension plan.

讓我們先從退休金方案開始。

❷ LET'S MOVE ON TO...

讓我們往下討論……（的部分）。

例 Let's move on to the subsidiary budget.

讓我們往下討論補貼預算的部分。

例 Let's move on to point three, the importance of first impressions.

讓我們往下討論第三點，第一印象的重要性。

❸ THAT BRINGS ME/US TO...

這把我／我們帶到……（的主題）。

例 That brings me to the topic of our merger.

這把我帶到我們合併案的主題上。

例 That brings us to the second point, the need for more volunteer service.

這把我們帶到第二點，增加義工服務的需求。

Word list

pension 〔`pɛnʃən〕 *n.* 退休金

subsidiary 〔səb`sɪdɪˌɛrɪ〕 *adj.* 補助的；次要的

Show Time

So, you can see from my comments that we really believe the Chinese market is the place to be. That brings us to the next topic, which is Asian political relations. Let me give you my thoughts about this.

如此，各位可以從我的說明了解到，我們深信中國市場是未來之所繫。這把我們帶到了下個主題，也就是亞洲政治關係。讓我向各位說明我對此的想法。

3.3 轉接 Transitioning

3.3a 強調 Highlighting

BIZ必通句型

❶ ...ESPECIALLY...

⋯⋯特別⋯⋯

例 The income of the potential customers is especially important.

潛在客戶的所得特別重要。

❷ ...IN PARTICULAR...

⋯⋯尤其⋯⋯

例 There are many things we should consider. In particular, we should consider how to lower the production costs.

有許多事情我們應該加以考慮。我們尤其應該考慮如何降低生產成本。

例 We have two problems. We must resolve the infrastructure problem, in particular.
我們有兩個問題。我們尤其必須解決基礎結構的問題。

❸ **MOST NOTABLE IS...**
最顯著的是……
例 Several factors have influenced our decision to cut back our production. Most notable is the recent stock market fall in the U.S.
我們減產的決定受到幾個因素的影響。最顯著的是最近美國股票市場大跌。

3.3b 一般性的說法 Generalizing

BIZ必通句型

❶ **...GENERALLY...**
……一般來說……
例 Generally, our managers have more than ten years of experience.
一般來說，我們的經理都擁有十年以上的經驗。
例 We generally submit the proposals one month in advance.
我們一般來說會在一個月之前提出計畫案。

❷ **AS A RULE...**
通常……
例 As a rule, the smaller shippers are better for us.
小型海運公司通常比較適合我們。

例 We don't offer such large discounts, as a rule.
我們通常不會提供這麼大的折扣。

3.3c 提供範例 Giving Examples

(*BIZ*必通句型)

❶ ...FOR EXAMPLE...
　　……例如……

例 There are many ways we can adapt the products to your needs. For example, we can change the color.
我們有許多方法可以讓產品符合您的需求。例如，我們可以改變顏色。

例 We want to think of ways to improve our business relationship. We might offer a longer contract, for example.
我們希望想出改善我們商業關係的方法。例如，我們可能會採較長期的合約。

❷ ...SUCH AS...
　　……諸如……

例 Our products are quite attractive to young people. They come in bright colors, such as red, pink, orange, and yellow.
我們的產品對年輕人相當具有吸引力。它們的顏色都很明亮，諸如紅色、粉紅色、橘色、以及黃色。

❸ ...FOR INSTANCE...
　　……譬如……

例 A number of factors prevented us from opening a factory in the central U.S. For instance, there is not enough water available for production.

有幾個因素使我們無法在美國中部設廠。譬如，沒有足夠生產所需的用水。

例 Our old director had several weaknesses. He didn't understand the environment, for instance.

我們以前的主管有幾個弱點。譬如，他對環境並不了解。

3.3d 說明原由 Giving Causes/Reasons

BIZ必通句型

❶ ...THEREFORE...

······因此······

例 The economy is not as stable as before. Therefore, we have to proceed carefully.

經濟沒有以前穩定。因此，我們必須更謹慎地進行。

❷ ...AS A RESULT...

······結果······

例 Costs have gone up. As a result, we must increase the price five percent.

成本業已上升。結果使得我們必須調漲價格百分之五。

❸ THE RESULT IS THAT...

結果是······

例 The wood we imported from Indonesia was improperly

stored.　The result is that the crates were not strong
enough.

我們從印尼進口的木材儲存不當。結果是做出來的板條箱不夠堅
固。

❹ **THAT'S WHY...**

這是為什麼……的原因。

例 Many customers have complained about the product.
That's why it has to be redesigned.

許多客戶對這項產品有諸多抱怨。這是為什麼它必須重新設計。

3.3e 反駁 Contradicting

*BIZ*必通句型

❶ **...ACTUALLY...**

……其實……

例 Actually, that is not the main reason.

其實,那並不是主要的原因。

例 We already tried that method, actually.

其實,我們已經試過了那個方法。

❷ **...IN FACT...**

……事實上……

例 In fact, it's not really possible.

事實上,這並不怎麼可能。

例 Our research shows the opposite, in fact.

事實上,我們的研究顯示正好相反。

3.3f 比較 Comparing

BIZ必通句型

❶ ...SIMILARLY...

⋯⋯同樣地⋯⋯

例 Our competitors' new models have the one-touch function. Similarly, our old model incorporates that special function.

我們競爭對手的新模型有單鍵操作的功能。同樣地,我們的舊款模型也具備那項特殊的功能。

❷ ...IN THE SAME WAY...

⋯⋯同樣地⋯⋯

例 The division in Vietnam has grown significantly in the last two years. In the same way, our China division can produce excellent results.

越南分部在過去兩年大幅成長。同樣地,我們在中國的分部也能有相當卓越的成績。

3.3g 轉入旁枝 Digressing

BIZ必通句型

❶ BY THE WAY...

對了 / 順便一提⋯⋯

Word list

incorporate〔ɪn`kɔrpə‚ret〕v. 使⋯⋯併入;包含

例 By the way, I'd like to mention our research subdivision.

對了，我想談一談我們的研究分部。

❷ **IN PASSING...**

順便一提……

例 In passing, I want to address our hiring policy.

順便提一下，我想討論我們的聘僱政策。

4 簡報的範例 Example Presentations

這個部分將會列舉一些實際的範例，讓各位了解以上說明的簡報用語應該如何整合起來。

了解了這些範例以及這些用語的應用方式，並大聲地複頌這些例句，會讓這些句子深深地烙印在你的腦海當中。

這個部分的範例是根據以下這個程序進行的演講。

簡報

公司介紹

1. 簡介
2. 主體
   A. 歷史
   B. 目前的產品
   C. 未來成長
3. 結語

4.1 簡介 Introduction

Show Time

Good afternoon. Welcome to Asia House, maker of high quality household cleaning products. I am very pleased to have you here today for our factory tour.

My name is Archer Lin. I am the marketing assistant here. Please feel free to call me Archer.

Before I take you on the tour, I want to give you a presentation. The purpose of the presentation is to provide you with some general information about the company so that you can better understand your factory tour.

The presentation should last about ten minutes. That is just long enough to give you enough information, and short enough to keep you from falling asleep!

My presentation has three parts. The first part is our company history. The second part is our current products. The third part is our future growth.

If you have a question, you can interrupt the presentation at any time.

午安，歡迎光臨亞洲屋，高品質家庭清潔產品的製造者。很高興各位今天能來我們工廠參觀。

我的名字是亞契‧林。我是這裡的行銷助理。請儘管叫我亞契。

在我帶領各位參觀之前，我想要先向各位作個簡報。這個簡報的目的是要提供各位一些有關本公司的基本資訊，這樣各位對本次工廠之行才會有更深刻的了解。

這個簡報將進行十分鐘。十分鐘的時間足夠讓各位獲得充分的資訊，卻不致於讓各位睡著！

我的簡報分三個部分。第一個部分是我們公司的歷史。第二個部分是我們目前的產品。第三個部分是我們未來的成長。

如果各位有問題的話，可以隨時打斷我的簡報。

4.2 主體的重點 A Main Topic in the Body

Show Time

That covers the first topic, company history. Let's move on to our current products, which is topic number two.

First, I want to tell you about our full range of products. Then, I will tell you more about our most famous product, the Double Clean reusable paper towel.

So, first, our range of products. We produce two kinds of products. One kind is cleaning sprays and liquids. We have a variety of cleaners for the bathroom, kitchen and living room. We have cleaners for every part of household cleaning, really. Our cleaners are perhaps best known for their nice fruit scents.

Next is our cloths and paper towels. Our company is known for producing cute paper towels and cleaning cloths. Each of our products has an impression of an animal: elephant, bear, seal, etc.

Our famous paper towel product is the Double Clean reusable paper towel. It comes in many different colors and is made of paper. Though it is made of paper, it can be used several hundred times. The technology to make the paper originated in Japan. We improved on the paper and made it even stronger. You will each receive a sample paper towel after a demonstration of its usage during the factory tour.

Let's leave the topic of current products. That brings me to the last topic, future growth.

這就是第一個主題的重點，公司歷史。接下來讓我們來談談我們目前的產品，這是第二個主題。

首先，我想向各位介紹我們的各種產品。之後，我會向各位介紹我們最知名的產品，「Double Clean」這種可重複使用的紙巾。

好，首先要講的是我們的各種產品。我們生產兩類產品。一類是清潔噴霧劑和清潔液。我們有各式各樣浴室、廚房、客廳的清潔用品。其實，我們有可以運用在家庭每個部分的清潔產品。我們的清潔產品最知名之處應該是清新的水果香味。

接下來要介紹的是我們的毛巾和紙巾。我們公司以生產可愛的紙巾和毛巾聞名。我們每項產品都印有動物的圖案：大象、熊、海狗等等。

我們最知名的紙巾產品是「Double Clean」這種可重複使用紙巾。它有許多不同的顏色，而且是用紙製造的。雖然它是用紙做的，但是可以重複使用好幾百次。製造這種紙巾的技術起源於日本。我們對材料紙加以改良，使它更加的耐用。各位在看過這項產品的使用示範之後都會獲得一份樣品。

讓我們將目前的產品這個主題告一段落。這帶我進入最後一個主題，未來的成長。

4.3 總結 Conclusion

Show Time

That concludes the main points of my presentation.

Now I would like to summarize the main topics. I have told you some basic information about our company history; the main point is that our company is fifteen years old, the oldest such company in Taiwan. Next, I explained our current products. The main product is our well-known

Double Clean reusable paper towel. The third topic is our future growth, and I tried to give you a general idea of the ways in which we want to enter the American market.

I hope you have a good general idea of our company now so that you can understand and appreciate your factory tour.

Thank you for your attention. I would be happy to answer any questions you might have.

以上就是我簡報的重點。

現在我想要為這些重點作個總結。我剛剛告訴各位一些我們公司歷史的基本資訊；重點是我們公司有十五年的歷史，是台灣同業當中歷史最悠久的公司。之後，我解說了我們目前的產品。我們主要的產品就是知名的 Double Clean 這種重複使用的紙巾。第三點是我們的未來成長，我試著讓各位對我們如何打入美國市場的方法有些概略的了解。

我希望各位現在對我們公司已有相當程度的了解，這樣各位在參觀工廠的時候就會有更深的體會。

謝謝各位的聆聽。我很樂意回答各位的問題。

Remember the Principles

1 簡報有其標準程序：簡介、主體、結論、以及發問和回答。這種簡報程序就像是機械的運作一般，每次都會產生同樣的結果。

Presentations have a standard process: introduction, body, conclusion, question and answer. The presentation process works like a machine, producing the same result every time.

2 最重要的是清晰傳達你的重點。這也是為什麼主要重點必須說三遍的原因：在簡介、在主體以及在結論的時候。

The most important thing is to make your main points clear. That is why the main points are stated three times: in the introduction, in the body, and in the conclusion.

5 實戰演練　Partner Practice

依照下列情境，找個同伴一起模擬對話，作爲實戰前的演練。

1 A是造訪海外的台灣人，B是該國人。雙方都在B的公司。

　　A：進行產品簡報。

　　（說明公司某項產品）

　　B：在簡報結束的時候提出問題。

　　以下是這個簡報可以使用的基本程序：

> 簡報
> X產品
> 1. 簡介
> 　　A. 問候
> 　　B. 自我介紹
> 　　C. 說明目的
> 　　D. 說明長度
> 　　E. 預先說明重點
> 　　F. 提問以及回答
> 2. 主體
> 　　A. 產品的使用
> 　　B. 產品的生產
> 　　　　1) 生產程序
> 　　　　2) 原料
> 　　C. 產品成本
> 3. 結論
> 　　A. 總結的開場白
> 　　B. 總結
> 　　C. 說明你的期許

> D. 結語
> 4. 發問以及回答

---

2 A是台灣人，B是造訪台灣的外國人。雙方在A的公司。

A：進行簡報介紹自己公司。

B：在簡報完畢後發問。

以下是這個簡報可以使用的基本程序：

> 簡報
> X產品
> 1. 簡介
>   A. 問候
>   B. 自我介紹
>   C. 說明目的
>   D. 說明長度
>   E. 預先說明重點
>   F. 提問以及回答
> 2. 主體
>   A. 公司歷史
>   B. 公司產品
>   1) 生產程序
>   2) 原料
>   3) 價格
>   C. 未來可能的發展
> 3. 結論
>   A. 總結的開場白
>   B. 總結
>   C. 說明你的期許
>   D. 結語
> 4. 發問以及回答

第 **6** 章

開會
Meetings

　　會議是正式商業溝通的骨幹。開會的目的是要做出決定、認識人們、分享想法、以及達成商業交易。如果各位了解基本的會議模式以及會議用語，就可以和西方人士成功地舉行會議。本章將會協助各位在邁向成功的大道上做好充分的準備。

　　Meetings are the backbone of formal business communication. Meetings are used to make decisions, get acquainted with people, share ideas, and reach business deals. If you know the basic meeting format and basic meeting language, you can have successful meetings with Western people. This chapter will set you on the road to success.

1 開會的說明 Talking about Meetings

各位需要先具備一些基本的字彙，才能在會議中有效溝通以及談論有關會議的事項。

1.1 基本字彙 Basic Vocabulary

記住以下的字彙。

*BIZ*必通字彙

正式群體溝通的類型 (Kinds of Formal Group Communication)
❶ conference〔`kɑnfərəns〕 *n.* 會議
❷ seminar〔`sɛmə,nɑr〕 *n.* 研討會
❸ meeting〔`mitɪŋ〕 *n.* 會議

人 (People)
❶ chairperson/chair〔`tʃɛr,pɝsn̩〕/〔tʃɛr〕 *n.* 主席
❷ secretary〔`sɛkrə,tɛrɪ〕 *n.* 秘書
❸ participant〔pə`tɪsəpənt〕 *n.* 參與者

★★★ *BIZ*一點通 ★★★

西方女性對性別的議題可能會相當地敏感。會議主席如果是女性可以稱為 Chairwoman，如果是男性則可以稱為 Chairman。男性和女性都可以稱為 Chair 或 Chairperson。不過不要稱女性主席為 Chairman!

討論事項 (Things to Discuss)

❶ item〔ˋaɪtəm〕 *n.* 事項

❷ topic〔ˋtɑpɪk〕/subject〔ˋsʌbdʒɪkt〕/matter〔ˋmætɚ〕
   n. 主題 / 題目 / 事務

❸ point〔pɔɪnt〕 *n.* 重點

❹ issue〔ˋɪʃju〕 *n.* 議題

會議記錄 (Meeting Records)

❶ minutes〔ˋmɪnɪts〕 *n.* 會議記錄

❷ proceedings〔prəˋsidɪŋz〕 *n.* 會議記錄

❸ report〔rɪˋport〕 *n.* 報告

★★★ *BIZ* 一點通 ★★★

Minutes（會議記錄）是指詳細的記錄，只有正式的重要會議，才需將與會人士以及相關決策做出詳細的記錄。
Proceedings（會議記錄）這種記錄是將與會人士所說的每個字都巨細靡遺地記錄下來，這種記錄方式唯有在政府會議以及法律程序當中較為常見。

1.2 配合情境的字彙 Vocabulary in Context

　　在以下 1.2 的部分有一些例句說明以上介紹的字彙。請各位大聲地複頌這些句子，重心放在這些例句當中字彙的用法。

1.2a 「正式群體溝通類型」的字彙
'Kinds of Formal Group Communication' Vocabulary

Show Time

❶ This is a very useful **conference**. I have learned a lot about sales techniques.

這是一場非常有用的會議。我學到許多有關銷售的技巧。

❷ My company always sends me to this yearly management **seminar**. They think it improves my management ability.

我公司總是派我來參加這一年一度的管理研討會。他們認為它能改善我的管理能力。

❸ Well, it is time for our weekly **meeting**. Who will start today?

嗯,我們週會的時間到了。今天由誰開始?

◇◇◇ 小心陷阱 ◇◇◇

☹ 錯誤用法

This is a very useful conference. I **had learned** a lot of things.

這是一場非常有用的會議。我學到許多事情。

☺ 正確用法

This is a very useful conference. I **have learned** a lot of things.

這是一場非常有用的會議。我學到許多事情。

◇◇◇ 小心陷阱 ◇◇◇

☹ 錯誤用法

My company always **send** me to this yearly seminar.

我公司總是派我來參加這一年一度的研討會。

☺ 正確用法

My company always **sends** me to this yearly seminar.

我公司總是派我來參加這一年一度的研討會。

1.2b 「參與者」的字彙 'People' Vocabulary

Show Time

❶ Phillip is not here today, so Joanne will serve as our **chair**.
菲利普今天不在這兒,所以瓊安會擔任我們的主席。

❷ We can start as soon as Mrs. Peterson, our **chairwoman**, arrives.
我們的主席彼得森太太一到後,我們就可以開始了。

❸ The boss is sick today. Would someone volunteer to be the **chairperson**?
老闆今天生病。有沒有人志願擔任主席?

❹ Each week we will ask one person at the meeting to serve as the **secretary**. That will be fair.
我們每個禮拜會要求一位與會人士擔任秘書,這樣才公平。

⑤ We have eight **participants** in tomorrow's meeting, so be sure to make eight copies of all the materials.
我們明天的會議有八位與會者,所以所有的資料務必都要印八份。

1.2c 「討論事項」的字彙 'Things to Discuss' Vocabulary

Show Time

❶ We will discuss four **items** in today's meeting.
我們今天的會議將會討論四個事項。

❷ We have two important **topics** to discuss.
我們有兩項重要的主題要討論。

❸ We have two important **subjects** to discuss.
我們有兩個重要的題目要討論。

❹ We have two important **matters** to discuss.
我們有兩件重要的事情要討論。

❺ I want to make two **points** before we continue.
在我們繼續之前,我想提出兩點。

❻ These **issues** are quite controversial, but we have to come up with some solutions.
這些議題相當具有爭議性,不過我們必須找出一些解決的辦法。

◇◇ 小心陷阱 ◇◇

☹ 錯誤用法

We have two important **topic** to discuss.

我們有兩個重要的主題要討論。

☺ 正確用法

We have two important **topics** to discuss.

我們有兩個重要的主題要討論。

1.2d 「會議紀錄」的字彙 'Meeting Records' Vocabulary

Show Time

❶ I don't remember who suggested that we write a new report. Can you check the **minutes** of last month's meeting to find out?

我不記得誰建議我們得撰寫新的報告。你能不能查查看上個月的會議記錄？

❷ We need to find out which legislator recommended the fee increase. See if you can get an official copy of the committee's **proceedings**.

我們必須知道是哪個立法委員建議調漲費用的。看看你能不能弄到一份該委員會的正式會議記錄。

Word list

come up with〔kʌm ʌp wɪð〕 *v.* 提出；想到

legislator〔ˋlɛdʒɪsˏletɚ〕 *n.* 立法委員

❸ After this meeting, the secretary will type up a **report** and distribute it to all the participants.
在這次會議之後，秘書會將報告打好，並且分發給所有的與會人士。

2 會議的基本要素　Basic Parts of a Meeting

各位得熟悉這些基本的會議要素。開會的基本模式和簡報一樣，請跟著以下這些基本的部分進行。

1. 會議的開場白
2. 進行會議
3. 會議的結語

下表是說明這三個基本部分的議程範例。

議程

行銷團隊月會

1. 開場白
2. 舊的議題
3. 新的議題
　　A. 新公司的行銷計畫
　　B. 新產品 L56 的目標市場
4. 結語

★★★ *BIZ* 一點通 ★★★

Item「事項」是說明會議議程的關鍵字。在以上的議程範例當中，有六個事項：1、2、3、3A、3B 以及 4。如「1.開場白」並不是一個 topic「主題」，也不是一個 point「重點」、或 subject「題目」，而是一個 item。

3 會議主席的特殊用語 Special Language for Chairs

會議主席在以上列舉的這三個會議環節分別需要用到一些特殊用語。這個部分列舉的都是協助會議主席達成以下兩種任務的特殊用語：

1. **會議的順利進行。（不要浪費時間。）**
   Keep moving forward. (Don't waste time.)
2. **專注在議程事項上。（不要一次談論一個以上的事項，免得造成混淆。）**
   Keep focused. (Don't confuse the meeting by talking about more than one item at one time.)

各位請注意，以下介紹的特殊用語有些和簡報的用語類似（甚至相同）。開會就好比舉行簡報一樣，會議主席就好比主導簡報的人。會議如果進行得順利，參與者會獲得充分的了解，而且感到滿意，正如聽了一場很棒的簡報一樣。

3.1 開場白 Language for Openings

會議開場白通常可以分成五個部分，每個部分都有其特殊的用語。這些部分包括：

1. 第一句話（告訴與會者會議開始）
2. 歡迎
3. 說明目的
4. 預先說明議程
5. 設定時間

除非特殊情況，否則順序通常如以上所示。

3.1a 第一個句子 First Sentence

BIZ必通句型

❶ LET'S BEGIN.
我們開始吧。

❷ LET'S GET DOWN TO BUSINESS.
我們開始討論正題吧。

❸ WE'D BETTER START.
我們最好開始。

❹ IT'S TIME TO BEGIN.
是開始的時候了。

❺ LET'S GET STARTED.
我們開始吧。

❻ SHALL WE BEGIN?
我們可以開始了嗎？

❼ OKAY/WELL/ALRIGHT...
好吧……
（可以用這些字來和緩開場白的句子）
例 Okay, let's begin.
好，我們開始吧。
例 Well, we'd better start.
嗯，我們最好開始。

3.1b 表達歡迎之意 Welcoming

BIZ必通句型

❶ WELCOME TO...
歡迎來到……
例 Welcome to our first monthly meeting of 2003!
歡迎來到我們2003年第一次月會。

❷ IT'S A PLEASURE TO WELCOME...
很高興歡迎……
例 It's a pleasure to welcome everyone to the meeting.
很高興歡迎大家來參加這次的會議。
例 It's a pleasure to welcome our special guests from Scotland.
很高興歡迎我們來自蘇格蘭的特別來賓。

❸ I WOULD LIKE TO START BY WELCOMING...
我想要先歡迎……
例 I would like to start by welcoming you all.
我想先對各位表達歡迎之意。
例 I would like to start by welcoming our new colleague, Miss Lee.
我想先對我們的新同事李小姐表達歡迎之意。

❹ I WOULD LIKE TO WELCOME...
我想要歡迎……
例 I would like to welcome our special friends who came all the way from Italy.
我想要歡迎我們遠從義大利而來的特別友人。

❺ LET ME BEGIN BY WELCOMING...

讓我從歡迎……開始。

例 Let me begin by welcoming you all to the first meeting for this quarter.

讓我先對各位來參加本季第一次會議表示歡迎之意。

❻ ON BEHALF OF..., I WOULD LIKE TO WELCOME...

作為……的代表，我要歡迎……

例 On behalf of our company, I would like to welcome all of our visitors.

僅代表我們公司，我要歡迎我們所有的來賓。

3.1c 說明會議的目的 Stating the Purpose

*BIZ*必通句型

❶ THE PURPOSE OF THIS MEETING IS TO...

這場會議的目的是……

例 The purpose of this meeting is to discuss some important issues related to our bankruptcy.

這場會議的目的是要討論和我們破產相關的一些重要議題。

❷ THE REASON WE ARE HERE IS TO...

我們聚在此地的原因是……

Word list

bankruptcy〔`bæŋkrʌptsɪ〕 *n.* 破產；倒閉

例 The reason we are here is to discuss ways to increase our revenue.
我們聚在此地的原因是要討論增加我們營收的方法。

❸ I HAVE CALLED THIS MEETING TO/SO THAT...
我召開這場會議是為了……

例 I have called this meeting to give us a chance to discuss the product launch.
我召開這場會議是為了讓我們有機會討論新產品的推出。

例 I have called this meeting so that we can go over the financial figures that were released yesterday.
我召開這場會議是為了討論昨天所發布的財務數字。

❹ AS YOU KNOW, WE ARE HERE TO...
誠如各位所知，我們聚在此地是為了……

例 As you know, we are here to decide a new sales campaign strategy.
誠如各位所知，我們聚在此地是為了決定新的銷售宣傳策略。

❺ WE ARE HERE TODAY TO...
我們今日聚在此地是為了……

例 We are here today to make a decision on the retirement plan.
我們今日聚在此地是為了對退休方案作出決定。

Word list

launch〔lɔntʃ〕 *n.*（新產品的）發售、推出
campaign〔kæmˋpen〕 *n.* 宣傳活動　　strategy〔ˋstrætədʒɪ〕 *n.* 戰略；策略

◇◇ 小心陷阱 ◇◇◇

☹ 錯誤用法

I have **opened** this meeting to introduce our new boss.

我召開這項會議是為了介紹我們的新老闆。

☺ 正確用法

I have **called** this meeting to introduce our new boss.

我召開這項會議是為了介紹我們的新老闆。

3.1d 預先說明議程 Previewing the Agenda

BIZ必通句型

❶ OUR AGENDA HAS...ITEMS. THEY ARE...

我們的議程有……項，分別是……

例 Our agenda has two items. They are the tax increase and the relocation of our Hong Kong factory.

我們的議程有兩項，分別是增稅問題和香港工廠的遷移事宜。

❷ AS YOU CAN SEE ON THE AGENDA...

誠如各位在議程表上所見……

例 As you can see on the agenda, we have three important matters to discuss today.

誠如各位在議程表上所看到的，我們今天有三項重要的事情要討論。

❸ LET'S PREVIEW THE AGENDA.

讓我們先看看議程。

例 Let's preview the agenda. We have four items to discuss today.

讓我們先看看議程。今天我們有四個討論事項。

❹ **LET'S TAKE A LOOK AT THE AGENDA.**
讓我們看看議程。

例 Let's take a look at the agenda. We will be discussing three main topics.

讓我們看看議程。我們將會討論三個主題。

◇◇◇ 小心陷阱 ◇◇◇

☹ 錯誤用法

As you **could** see on the agenda, we have many items today.

誠如各位在議程表上所見，我們今天有許多要討論的事項。

☺ 正確用法

As you **can** see on the agenda, we have many items today.

誠如各位在議程表上所見，我們今天有許多要討論的事項。

3.1e 設定時間 Setting the Time

BIZ 必通句型

❶ **THE MEETING WILL LAST...**
這場會議將進行……

例 The meeting will last thirty minutes.
這場會議將進行三十分鐘。

② THE MEETING WILL FINISH AT...
這會議將在⋯⋯結束。
例 The meeting will finish at 3:30.
這場會議將在三點半結束。

③ THE MEETING SHOULD END AT...
這場會議應該會在⋯⋯結束。
例 The meeting should end at 5:00.
這場會議應該會在五點鐘結束。

④ THE MEETING SHOULD FINISH BY...
這場會議應該會在⋯⋯前結束。
例 The meeting should finish by lunch time.
這場會議應該在午餐時間前結束。

⑤ THE MEETING SHOULD TAKE ABOUT...
這場會議應該會進行大約⋯⋯
例 This meeting should take about thirty minutes.
這會議應該會進行大約三十分鐘的時間。

⑥ LET'S AIM/SHOOT FOR A...FINISH.
讓我們預定⋯⋯時結束。
例 Let's aim for a 2:00 finish.
讓我們預定在兩點結束。
例 Let's shoot for an 11:30 finish.
讓我們預定在十一點半結束。

❼ WE WILL ONLY TAKE...

我們只會花……

例 We will only take twenty minutes.

我們只會花二十分鐘。

❽ WE ONLY HAVE...TODAY.

我們今天只有……

例 We only have thirty minutes today.

我們今天只有三十分鐘。

Show Time

It's nice to see all of you here again. Shall we begin?

It's a pleasure to welcome our newcomers to this meeting. I guess you have met everyone already. We are happy to have you with us.

As you know, we are here to decide the issues to be discussed at our upcoming sales conference. I have a list of all the issues that you all have submitted to me, and we will be discussing which ones are most important. I am sure we will have a fruitful discussion.

Let's take a quick look at the agenda. There are only three items. The first item is: review of all the issues. The second item is: selection of the most important issues. And the final item is: deciding which issues are to be on the first day of the conference, and which issues are to be on the second day of the conference.

Word list

submit〔səb`mɪt〕 v. 提出　　fruitful〔`frutfəl〕 adj. 收穫多的；有益的

Let's shoot for a noon finish so that we can all have lunch together.

- -

能在這兒再度和各位見面真好。我們可以開始了嗎？

很高興歡迎我們的新人來參加這次的會議。我想你已經和每個人都見過面了。我們很高興你能夠加入我們的行列。

誠如各位所知，我們在此要決定即將舉行的銷售會議中將討論的相關議題。我有一份各位所提出的議題清單，我們將會討論其中哪些最為重要。我很確定我們會有很豐碩的結果。

讓我們很快地看看議程。當中只有三個事項。第一項是：檢視所有的議題。第二項是：選擇最重要的議題。最後一項是：決定哪個事項必須在會議第一天討論，哪些議題在會議的第二天討論。

讓我們預定在中午結束，這樣我們可以一塊用午餐。

3.2 進入主題的用語 Language for Going through Business

對於西方人而言，開會是為了達成商業上的目的。西方的會議鮮少是為了建立關係而召開的。確定會議成功地達成商業上的任務是會議主席的責任。與會者會期待主席直接、清晰地帶領討論每一項議題。

3.2a 說明討論事項的開場白 Opening an Item

BIZ必通句型

❶ **THE FIRST ITEM IS...**

第一項是……

例 The first item is our travel stipend policy.

第一項是我們的出差費政策。

❷ LET'S BEGIN WITH...

讓我們從……開始。

例 Let's begin with the first item.

讓我們從第一項開始。

例 Let's begin with the topic of our budget deficit.

讓我們從預算赤字的主題開始討論。

❸ THE NEXT ITEM IS...

下個事項是……

例 The next item is our office redecoration.

下個事項是我們辦公室重新裝潢的議題。

❹ THE...ITEM IS...

第……項是……

例 The second item is salary cuts.

第二項是減薪的議題。

例 The fourth item is the recent shipping delays.

第四項是最近貨運延誤的問題。

❺ THE LAST/FINAL ITEM IS...

最後一個事項是……

例 The last item is the purchase of new computer
equipment.

最後一項是採購新電腦設備的議題。

例 The final item is our end-of-year party.

最後一項是我們年底的派對。

Word list

stipend〔`staɪpɛnd〕 *n.* 津貼；薪俸

❻ LET'S MOVE ON TO THE...ITEM.

讓我們繼續進入第……項。

例 Let's move on to the next item.

讓我們繼續進入下個事項。

例 Let's move on to the third item.

讓我們繼續進入第三項。

❼ NOW WE COME TO THE...ITEM.

現在我們來到第……項。

例 Now we come to the second item.

現在我們來到第二項。

例 Now we come to the last item.

現在我們來到最後一項。

3.2b 焦點集中在討論主題上 Focusing on an Item

帶領大家逐項討論是會議主席的責任。與會人士往往會偏離主題、討論一些別的事情。當這樣的情況發生時，主席必須把與會者帶回討論事項。

*BIZ*必通句型

❶ LET'S COME BACK TO...

讓我們回到……

例 Let's come back to item two. We can talk about your idea later.

讓我們回到第二項。我們可以稍後再討論你的點子。

❷ LET'S GET BACK TO...

讓我們回到……

例 That is an interesting point, but let's get back to our topic.

那論點很有意思，不過讓我們回到我們討論的主題。

❸ CAN WE COME BACK TO...?

我們可以回到……嗎？

例 Can we come back to the topic of international air freight? We will discuss domestic transportation later.

我們可以回到國際空運的主題嗎？我們將於稍後討論國內運輸的議題。

❹ CAN WE GET BACK TO...?

我們可以回到……嗎？

例 Can we get back to the issue of item three? We need to finish discussing this.

我們可以回到第三項的議題嗎？我們得把這個討論完畢。

❺ LET'S JUST DEAL WITH...

讓我們只處理……

例 Let's just deal with the cost right now. We can discuss your other concerns later.

讓我們現在只處理成本的議題。我們可以稍後再討論其它你們關切的議題。

❻ WE WILL GET TO...LATER.

我們稍後會回到……

例 We will get to that subject later.

我們稍後會回到那個議題。

◇◇◇ 小心陷阱 ◇◇◇

☹ 錯誤用法

Let's **back** to our topic.

讓我們回到我們的主題。

☺ 正確用法

Let's **get back** to our topic.

讓我們回到我們的主題。

Show Time

Chair : Alright, let's begin with the topic of technology upgrade in our factory assembly line. Is it a good idea or not?

Participant : That reminds me of the high cost of voice mail systems. That voice mail system is just too expensive, and I suggest we go back to our old phone system.

Chair : That's an important issue, and we will talk about that in next week's meeting. Right now let's get back to the topic of technology upgrade in our factory.

Participant : Oh, alright.

會議主席：好的，讓我們開始討論我們工廠組裝線技術升級的主題。這個點子好不好呢？

與會者 ：這讓我想起高成本的語音郵件系統。這個語音郵件系統實在過於昂貴，我建議我們應該回頭採用原來的電話系統。

會議主席：那個議題很重要，我們將會在下個禮拜的會議當中進行討論。現在讓我們回到我們工廠技術升級的議題。

與會者 ：喔，好的。

3.2c 結束某個事項的討論 Closing an Item

BIZ必通句型

❶ THAT'S ALL FOR...

……的討論完畢。

例 That's all for item three.

第三項的討論完畢。

❷ THAT COVERS...

那涵蓋了……

例 Well, that covers the second issue.

嗯,那涵蓋了第二項議題。

❸ THAT BRINGS US TO THE END OF...

那帶我們進入……的尾聲。

例 That brings us to the end of the last item.

那帶我們進入最後一項的尾聲。

❹ LET'S LEAVE...

讓我們停止討論……

例 I guess nobody has anything else to say. Let's leave item three.

我想大家都已經沒有別的要說的了,讓我們停止討論第三項。

❺ LET'S MOVE ON.

讓我們繼續。

◇◇◇ 小心陷阱 ◇◇◇

☹ 錯誤用法

That **is cover** item one.

那涵蓋了第一項的討論。

☺ 正確用法

That **covers** item one.

那涵蓋了第一項的討論。

3.2d 進入下個討論主題 Moving to the Next Item

BIZ 必通句型

❶ LET'S MOVE ON TO...

讓我們接著進行……

例 Let's move on to item two.

讓我們接著討論第二項。

例 Let's move on to the next item.

讓我們接著討論下一個事項。

❷ LET'S GO TO THE...ITEM.

讓我們進行……事項。

例 Let's go to the next item.

讓我們進行下個事項。

例 Let's go to the last item.

讓我們進行最後一個事項。

❸ LET'S GO TO ITEM...

讓我們進行……項。

例 Let's go to item four.
讓我們進行第四項。

❹ SHALL WE MOVE ON TO...?
我們接著進行……項好嗎？
例 Shall we move on to item two?
我們接著進行第二項好嗎？
例 Shall we move on to the last item?
我們接著進行最後第一項好嗎？

Show Time

Okay, we have had some good ideas about how to proceed with our new products. So, let's leave that item. Shall we move on to item three? Who would like to begin the discussion?

好，我們對於新產品要如何去進行已經有些不錯的點子。所以，讓我們停止討論這個事項。我們繼續進入第三項好嗎？誰想先開始討論？

3.3 結束會議的用語 Language for Closings

　　良好的結語可讓會議參與者覺得會議進行得很順利。就好像飛機落地一般，大家都會對圓滿的結尾感到高興。會議主席需要遵循以下這幾個步驟，才能順暢地為會議畫下休止符。

　　1. 摘要說明
　　2. 確定大家都了解無誤
　　3. 最後一句話

3.3a 摘要說明 Summarizing

*BIZ*必通句型

❶ LET'S SUM UP.
讓我們進行總結。

❷ LET'S SUMMARIZE.
讓我們進行總結。

❸ LET'S GO OVER THE MAIN POINTS AGAIN.
讓我們重複一下幾個要點。

❹ LET'S RECAP.
讓我們重述要點。

3.3b 確定大家都了解無誤 Ensuring Clarity

*BIZ*必通句型

❶ IS EVERYTHING CLEAR?
所有的事情都很清楚了嗎？

❷ DOES ANYONE HAVE ANY QUESTIONS?
有人有問題嗎？

❸ DOES EVERYTHING MAKE SENSE?
每個事項是否都合理？

❹ IS THERE ANYTHING I CAN CLARIFY?
有沒有需要我說明的地方？

◇◇◇ 小心陷阱 ◇◇◇

☹ 錯誤用法
Is anyone have any questions?
有人有問題嗎？

☺ 正確用法
Does anyone have any questions?
有人有問題嗎？

3.3c 最後一句話 Final Sentence

BIZ 必通句型

❶ LET'S CALL IT A DAY.
我們今天就到此為止。

❷ LET'S STOP HERE.
我們在此告一段落。

❸ LET'S END HERE.
我們在此結束。

❹ LET'S FINISH HERE.
我們在此結束。

❺ I BELIEVE WE'RE FINISHED.
我相信我們已經討論完畢。

❻ WE'LL STOP HERE FOR TODAY.
我們今天在此告一段落。

◇◇◇ 小心陷阱 ◇◇◇

☹ 錯誤用法
I believe we are **finish**.
我認為我們已經討論完畢。

☺ 正確用法
I believe we are **finished**.
我認為我們已經討論完畢。

(Show Time)

Thanks for all of your contributions in this meeting. I think we have heard some important ideas today. Now, let's sum up. We only had two items of business today. The first item was the recent failures in the assembly line. I think we have figured out how to solve that problem. The second item was the brainstorm of styles for our new line of shirts. We have many ideas now and will have another meeting soon to select the best ones.

Is there anything I can clarify? [Pause.] Good. I guess everything is clear.

I believe we're finished, then.

謝謝大家在這次會議中的貢獻。我想我們今天聽到了一些重要的想法。現在，進行總結。我們今天討論的只有兩個事項。第一個事項是最近組裝線上的失誤。我認為我們已經想出解決問題的方法。第二個項目是為我們新款的襯衫式樣進行腦力激盪。我們現在有許多點子，近期會再度舉行會議從中挑選最好的。

有沒有需要我說明的地方？〔停頓一下〕很好，我想所有的事情都很清楚了。

　　那，我認為我們已經討論完畢了。

4 與會人士的特殊用語
Special Language for Participants

與會者有責任要投入會議！主席會確保會議進行得順暢、直接、清楚、有效率，這樣與會者才能充分地進行討論，並且有效地貢獻意見。記住，西方人會期望所有與會人士的參與，每個人都應該貢獻以及分享他們的點子。以下這些用語可以讓各位以有效的方法參與會議。

4.1 插話的用語 Language for Interrupting

插話的技巧相當重要。在西方的文化當中，打斷別人講話有兩個重要的原則：

1. 所有的人都可以打斷其他與會者的講話。

2. 被打斷的人可以制止這樣的行為，並且繼續講下去。

如果你有什麼重要的事情要說，可以隨時打斷其他與會者的談話。不過被打斷的人也可以制止你。如果你打斷某個人的講話，對方不會感到生氣。同樣的，如果對方制止你打斷他的講話，你也不應該感到不高興。西方人在開會的時候會隨時打斷別人講話、或是制止別人打斷他們講話！這並沒有什麼好怕的，人們也不會因此而生氣。西方人開會的風格是確保每個人都有機會表達他們想要／需要說的話。

台灣人對於打斷其他與會者談話往往覺得很不舒服，但當別人打斷他們講話的時候，卻又不敢制止。首先，別害怕打斷別人講話，或是制止別人打斷你的談話。在西方文化裡，這兩者都是你的權力。這個部分將會介紹各位如何妥當地運用插話的用語。

4.1a 插話的用語 Interrupting

BIZ必通句型

❶ **MAY I INTERRUPT?**
我可以插句話嗎？

❷ **CAN I SAY SOMETHING HERE?**
這裡我可以說句話嗎？

❸ **I'D LIKE TO SAY SOMETHING HERE.**
我想要在這裡說句話。

❹ **JUST A MOMENT.**
等一下。

❺ **SORRY/EXCUSE ME...**
對不起……
（你在打斷別人講話的時候，最好先說句對不起）
例 Sorry, Mrs. Streisand, can I say something here?
對不起，史翠珊得女士，我可以在這裡說句話嗎？
例 Excuse me, I'd like to say something here.
對不起，我想在這裡說句話。

Show Time

Participant A: I would like to comment on that point. We definitely cannot afford to introduce a new clothing line now. We already have a debt problem that...

Participant B: Sorry, may I interrupt? I just want to point out
　　　　　　　that we paid our debt yesterday and don't
　　　　　　　have a budget deficit any more.

與會者A：我想要對那點作個說明。我們現在絕對無法負擔推出新
　　　　　款的衣服。我們已經有債務的問題……
與會者B：對不起，我可以打一下岔嗎？我只是要指出我們昨天已
　　　　　經償還債務，已經沒有預算赤字的問題了。

4.1b 阻止他人插話 Stopping Interruptions

*BIZ*必通句型

❶ MAY I JUST FINISH?
我可以講完嗎？

❷ IF I CAN JUST FINISH.
如果我可以講完的話。

❸ LET ME FINISH WHAT I WAS SAYING.
讓我把話講完。

❹ I'D LIKE TO FINISH.
我想講完。

❺ LET ME FINISH FIRST.
讓我先講完。

◇◇◇ 小心陷阱 ◇◇◇

☹ 錯誤用法

Let me finish what I was **said**.

讓我把話講完。

☺ 正確用法

Let me finish what I was **saying**.

讓我把話講完。

Show Time

Participant A: I agree with Fred. Barney's department has got to make some cutbacks. The department spends too much unnecessary money. That money...

Participant B: Can I say something here?

Participant A: Let me finish what I was saying.

Participant B: Okay.

Participant A: That money could be used for the new advertising campaign...

參與者A：我同意佛瑞德的意見。巴尼的部門必須進行縮編。這個部門花太多沒有必要的錢。那些錢……

與會者B：這裡我可以說句話嗎？

參與者A：讓我把話講完。

參與者B：好。

參與者A：那些錢可以花在新的廣告活動上……

Word list

cutback〔`kʌt,bæk〕 *n.* 削減；裁減

4.2 表達意見的用語 Language for Expressing Opinions

記住，西方人想要聽取每個與會者的意見。所以，儘管自我表達！提供你的意見、點子、以及建議。如果你參與會議，你就是這個會議重要的一部分！

4.2a 發表看法 Offering Opinions

BIZ必通句型

❶ I THINK...

我想……

例 I think we should use the leftover money to buy something we need.

我想我們應該利用剩下來的錢去買我們需要的東西。

❷ I BELIEVE...

我相信……

例 I believe this project cannot succeed if we do not increase the manpower.

我相信如果我們不增加人力的話，這個專案就不會成功。

★★★ *BIZ* 一點通 ★★★

Believe「相信」這個字眼比 think「認為」語氣上強烈一些。

❸ IN MY OPINION...

依我看……

例 In my opinion, the color should be changed to green.

依我看，這個顏色應該改成綠色。

❹ IN MY VIEW...

依我看……

例 In my view, the color should be changed to green.

依我看，這個顏色應該改成綠色。

❺ AS FAR AS I KNOW, ...

就我所知……

例 As far as I know, the air cargo system to England is very good.

就我所知，到英國的空運系統相當好。

❻ ACCORDING TO MY CALCULATIONS, ...

根據我的計算，……

例 According to my calculations, it is not really economical to hire so many workers from outside our city.

根據我的計算，聘僱這麼多外縣市的員工實在不合算。

❼ IT SEEMS TO ME THAT...

在我看來似乎……

例 It seems to me that we are focusing too much attention on the production process.

在我看來我們似乎太過專注在生產流程。

❽ ACCORDING TO MY EXPERIENCE, ...

根據我的經驗，……

例 According to my experience, one large shipment is better than two small shipments.

根據我的經驗，一次大量的裝運要比分成兩小批好。

❾ THE WAY I SEE IT, ...

在我看來……

例 The way I see it, we need to retrain our older employees.

在我看來，我們需要重新訓練較為年長的員工。

◇◇◇ 小心陷阱 ◇◇◇

☹ 錯誤用法

As I know, that is not possible.

就我所知，那是不可能的。

☺ 正確用法

As far as I know, that is not possible.

就我所知，那是不可能的。

★★★ BIZ一點通 ★★★

許多西方人用 feel「感覺」這個字，來表示 think「認為」的意思。如：I feel this is a good idea.（我覺得這是個好點子。）然而，頂尖的專業人士不會這麼說。「認為」和「感覺」並不一樣。

例 I feel happy.

我覺得高興。

例 I feel depressed.

我覺得消沉。

以上是使用 feel 的好方法。不過如果說 I feel this is a bad idea.（我覺得這是個壞點子。）就不合邏輯了。你應該說：

例 I think this is a bad idea.

我認為這是個壞點子。

頂尖的專業人士會適當地用詞遣字。

4.2b 對於他人看法發表評論 Commenting on Others' Opinions

BIZ必通句型

❶ THAT'S A GOOD/GREAT...
那是個很好的……
例 That's a good point.
那是個很好的論點。
例 That's a great idea!
那是個很棒的點子！

❷ THAT'S INTERESTING.
那很有意思。

❸ I NEVER THOUGHT OF THAT.
我從來沒有想到過那個。

❹ THAT'S A NOVEL IDEA.
那是個很新的點子。

Show Time

Participant A: In my view, the spare parts we are importing from France are too expensive. We can purchase the same parts from Italy at a better price. Also, we can save shipping costs by shipping them with the other supplies we already purchase in Italy.

Participant B: I never thought of that.

與會者 A：在我看來，我們從法國進口的零件太過昂貴。我們可以
用更好的價格在義大利買到同樣的零件。而且，連同其
他我們已經向義大利採購的物品一塊運送，還可以節省
貨運成本。

與會者 B：我從來沒有想到那點。

4.2c 表達認同 Agreeing

BIZ必通句型

❶ I AGREE (WITH)...

我同意……

例 I agree with your suggestion.

我同意你的建議。

❷ I COMPLETELY/TOTALLY AGREE (WITH)...

我完全認同……

例 I totally agree with Joshua's opinion.

我完全認同約書亞的意見。

例 I completely agree!

我完全認同！

❸ I'M WITH YOU.

我同意你的說法。

❹ I COULDN'T AGREE MORE.

我完全認同。

❺ I AGREE ONE HUNDRED PERCENT.

我百分之一百的認同。

◇◇◇ 小心陷阱 ◇◇◇

☹ 錯誤用法

I **agree** you.

我認同你的說法。

☺ 正確用法

I **agree with** you.

我認同你的說法。

4.2d 表達不認同 Disagreeing

BIZ必通句型

❶ I DISAGREE (WITH)...

我不認同……

例 I disagree with your estimates.

我不認同你的估計。

❷ I COMPLETELY/TOTALLY DISAGREE (WITH)...

我完全不認同……

例 Elizabeth, I completely disagree with Mr. Gould's assessment.

伊麗莎白，我完全不認同古德先生的評估。

例 I totally disagree with those estimates.

我完全不認同這些估計。

❸ I'M NOT WITH YOU.

我不認同你的說法。

❹ I COULDN'T DISAGREE MORE.
我徹底地不認同。

❺ I COULDN'T AGREE LESS.
我完完全全不認同。

❻ I DISAGREE ONE HUNDRED PERCENT.
我百分之一百的不認同。

Show Time

❶ Participant A: According to my experience, the soft colors are more popular than the bright colors.
Participant B: I agree one hundred percent. The bright colors never sell as well.

與會者A：根據我的經驗，柔和的顏色比明亮的顏色更受歡迎。
與會者B：我百分之一百的同意。明亮的顏色向來都沒有柔和的顏色賣得好。

❷ Participant A: I believe we should wait a few years before modifying our most popular products.
Participant B: I'm not with you. If we want to remain competitive, we have to continually upgrade our products.

與會者A：我認為我們應該等個幾年，然後才調整我們最受歡迎的產品。
與會者B：我不同意你的說法。如果我們想要維持競爭力，就必須持續不斷地讓產品升級。

4.2e 表示理解對方 Showing Understanding

以下這些用語並不表示你同意。只是表示你了解對方所說的話。

BIZ必通句型

❶ I FOLLOW YOU.
我懂你的意思。

❷ I GOT YOU.
我懂了。

❸ I SEE ...'S POINT.
我了解⋯⋯的觀點。
例 I see Heather's point.
　 我了解海瑟的觀點。

❹ I SEE WHAT YOU MEAN.
我了解你的意思。

◇◇◇ 小心陷阱 ◇◇◇

☹ 錯誤用法
　 I see you mean.
　 我了解你的意思。
☺ 正確用法
　 I see **what** you mean.
　 我了解你的意思。

Show Time

Participant A: I don't think we can move into the American market at this time. We'd better secure more financial resources first.

Participant B: I follow you.

Participant A: The import-export bank will probably help us if we need help, but before that we should build our capital reserves.

Participant B: I see what you mean.

Participant A: So, do you agree we shouldn't move into the American market now?

Participant B: Actually, I completely disagree. I think we have to move now, or we will lose our chance forever.

與會者A：我不認為我們這時候可以進軍美國市場。我們最好先取得更多的財務資源。

與會者B：我懂你的意思。

與會者A：如果我們需要協助的話，進出口銀行可能會協助我們，不過在這之前，我們應該儲備自己的資本。

與會者B：我了解你的意思。

與會者A：那，你同意我們這時候不應該進軍美國市場嗎？

與會者B：事實上，我完全不同意。我認為我們應該現在行動，否則就會永遠喪失我們的機會。

4.3 提出問題的用語 Language for Asking Questions

提問用語是很有用處的。如果你在開會時有不了解的地方，請提出

你的問題！西方人喜歡別人提問。提問可以讓別人知道你真心想要了解。

4.3a 要求更多資訊 Seeking More Information

❶ COULD YOU TELL (ME/US) MORE ABOUT...?
您可以告訴（我／我們）更多有關於⋯⋯？
例 Could you tell me more about the cost advantages?
您可以告訴我更多有關於成本優勢的事嗎？

❷ COULD YOU EXPLAIN MORE ABOUT...?
您可否進一步解釋⋯⋯？
例 Could you explain more about the product specifications?
您可否進一步解釋產品規格？

❸ I'D LIKE TO KNOW MORE ABOUT...
我想要進一步了解有關⋯⋯
例 I'd like to know more about your outsourcing.
我想要進一步了解您委外的事宜。

❹ I'D LIKE TO HAVE MORE INFORMATION.
我想要有更多的資訊。

❺ COULD YOU EXPAND ON THAT?
您可否針對那點加以解釋？

◇◇◇ 小心陷阱 ◇◇◇

☹ 錯誤用法

I like to know more about that.

我想要進一步了解有關那方面的事。

☺ 正確用法

I would like/I'd like to know more about that.

我想要進一步了解有關那方面的事。

4.3b 要求說明 Seeking Clarity

BIZ必通句型

❶ WHAT DO YOU MEAN BY/WHEN...

你說……是什麼意思？

例 What do you mean by that?

你說那是什麼意思？

例 What do you mean we cannot predict the future?

你說我們無法預測未來是什麼意思？

❷ COULD YOU REPHRASE THAT?

您可否換個方式再說一次？

❸ COULD YOU EXPLAIN THAT ?

您可否對那件事加以解釋？

Word list

rephrase〔rɪ`frez〕v. 改變措辭表達

❹ **I'M NOT CLEAR ON...**
我對⋯⋯並不了解。
例 I'm not clear on your explanation of the style differences.
我並不了解你對款式差異的說明。

❺ **I'M NOT SURE I UNDERSTAND...**
我不確定是否了解⋯⋯
例 I'm not sure I understand your point about the changing trend.
我不確定是否了解你對正在改變的潮流的說法。

❻ **I'M NOT SURE WHAT YOU MEAN.**
我不確定你的意思。

Show Time

Participant A: Our product range is just too big. We need to be more focused.
Participant B: What do you mean by "focused"?
Participant A: I mean that we should take our most popular products and try to produce products in only those lines. We can focus on those lines.
Participant B: Okay. I see what you mean. Can you explain more about dropping some of our product lines?

與會者A：我們的產品範疇太大。我們需要更加專精。
與會者B：你說「更加專精」是什麼意思？
與會者A：我的意思是，我們應該選擇最受歡迎的產品，試著只生產這些系列的產品。我們可以專注在這些系列上。

與會者 B：好，我了解你的意思。你可否進一步說明有關放棄我們
部分系列產品的看法？

5 會議的範例　More Meeting Examples

5.1 開場白　Opening

以下 Show Time 單元中的範例，乃是依造下列的議程來進行。

> 議程
> 工程團隊週會
> 1. 開場白
> 2. 進入主題
>   A. 錯誤評估實驗室的修繕
>   B. L501 晶片設計團隊
> 3. 宣佈事項
> 4. 結語

Show Time

　　Well, we better start. I would like to start by welcoming everyone. This is the first meeting in our new series of weekly meetings just for the engineers. Some of you have been asking for a regular meeting for a long time, so I am sure you are eager to get started. I hope these meetings will be beneficial.

　　The reason we are here today is to discuss the two most important issues we will be dealing with next month. Most of you have asked me to include these on the agenda, and I have done so. As you can see on the agenda, these issues are: One, the renovation of our error assessment lab; and, Two, the selection of the design team for our future L501 chip.

The meeting will finish at noon. That gives us two hours. Ordinarily, the meetings will last only one hour. But I think this first meeting will require a lot of discussion, since you are all eager to discuss the two issues on the agenda. So, let's begin with the first item of business: error assessment lab renovation. Let's begin by going around the table and getting everyone's opinion before we have free discussion.

嗯，我們最好開始。一開始我要向各位表達歡迎之意。在我們專為工程師召開一連串新的週會中，這是第一場會議。各位當中有些人長久以來一直要求要召開例行性會議，所以我確定各位一定很想趕快開始。我希望這些會議能讓各位有豐富的收穫。

我們今天聚在這裡的原因是為了要討論我們下個月得處理的兩項最重要議題。你們大多數人都要求我把這些事項列入議程，而我也照辦了。誠如各位在議程表上所見，這些議題分別是：第一，我們「錯誤評估實驗室」的修繕；第二，選出我們未來的L501晶片設計團隊。

這場會議將會在中午的時候結束。換言之，我們有兩個小時的時間。一般來說，這些會議只會持續一個小時。不過我認為這頭一場會議需要許多的討論，因為各位都很希望討論議程上的這兩項議題。所以，讓我們由第一事項開始：「錯誤評估實驗室」的修繕。在自由討論前，我們先繞桌子一圈，聽聽每個人的意見。

Word list

renovation〔͵rɛnəˋveʃən〕 n. 修繕；革新
assessment〔əˋsɛsmənt〕 n. 評估；估價

5.2 結語 Closing

以下 Show Time 單元中的範例，乃是延續 5.1 的議程來進行。

Show Time

We have had some very interesting discussion. Well, it is almost noon now, so let's go over the main points again. First, the renovation of the error assessment lab. All of you agree that the lab needs to be renovated. Some of you even think there are a few fire hazards in the lab. So, I will take your specific ideas to the President tomorrow. Second, the design team for the L501 chip. Henry, you have agreed to head up the team. Beatrice is in charge of soliciting nominations for the design team. The list of nominations will be given to me next Monday, and I will choose the three members for Henry's team.

Does anyone have any questions? [Pause.] No? Okay, then I guess everything is clear. Let's stop here, then.

我們的討論非常有意思。嗯，現在幾乎快要中午了，所以，讓我們回顧一下幾個重點。首先，「錯誤評估實驗室」的修繕。各位都同意實驗室需要修繕。有些人甚至認為實驗室可能有發生火警的危險。所以，我明天會將各位明確的意見提交總裁。第二，L501 晶片設計團隊。亨利，你同意帶領這個團隊。碧翠斯負責找設計團

Word list

solicit〔sə`lɪsɪt〕 v. 懇求；央求
nomination〔ˌnɑmə`neʃən〕 n. 提名；任命

隊的可能成員。提名名單下禮拜一交給我，我將為亨利的團隊選出三位成員。

　　有沒有人有問題？〔停頓一下〕沒有嗎？好，我想所有的事情都很清楚了。那麼，我們在此散會。

5.3 事項的討論過程 An Item of Business

> 議程
> 聘僱委員會的特殊會議
> 1. 開場白
> 2. 進入主題
> 　　A. 要聘僱多少人
> 　　B. 求職者的選擇
> 3. 結語

　　根據上列會議環節中「進入主題」的部分，以下的範例是四個與會人士的對話：主席、安妮、貝蒂、以及凱文。

Show Time

Chair: Okay, that covers Item 2A: the number of people to hire. About eighty percent of us agree that we should hire two people. Let's move on to the next item of business, 2B: selection of candidates. Everyone has the resume of each candidate and has had time to read all of the resumes. We have to choose two candidates. Let's start the discussion by taking any comments anyone has to offer. Maybe it will be that the two best candidates will come to the front right away. So, who would like to start?

主席：好的，這涵蓋了 2A 事項的討論：聘僱人數。我們當中大約百分之八十的人同意應該聘用二人。

讓我們進入下個討論事項 2B ：挑選人選。每個人都有一份求職者的履歷表，並有時間讀過所有的履歷。我們必須選出兩個人。討論一開始，先讓我們聽聽各位的意見。說不定我們可以立即從中找到最好的人選。所以，誰想要開始？

Annie: I think we should hire the two candidates from the International Trade Institute in Hsinchu. Their language and business training seems to be better than the candidates with bachelor's degrees in business.

安妮：我認為我們應該選來自新竹的國貿學院的兩位。他們的語言能力以及商業訓練似乎都比具有商學院學士學位的求職者要強。

Calvin: I agree with Annie that those two candidates are well qualified, but I am reluctant to hire two people from the same school. I believe it is better to have new people who do not know each other.

凱文：我同意安妮的意見，那兩位求職者都相當符合條件，不過我覺得不應該聘用同一所學校的兩個人。我認為最好僱用兩個彼此不認識的新人。

Betty: You are reluctant to hire people from the same school? What do you mean by that?

貝蒂：你不願意僱用同一所學校的兩個人？你這麼說是什麼意思？

Chair: Yes. Could you explain more about that?
主席：是的，你能不能進一步說明？

Calvin: It's okay if they are from the same school. I am reluctant if they graduated at the same time, which means they know each other. I think people grow up in a company faster if they don't have someone to attach themselves to for comfort.
凱文：如果他們來自同一所學校沒關係。不過如果他們是同一年的畢業生，那就不好，因為這表示他們彼此認識。我認為，新人如果沒有可以依賴、尋求慰藉的對象，在公司的成長速度會比較快。

Betty: I see your point. Well, who would you suggest as candidates then, Calvin?
貝蒂：我了解你的意思。嗯，那你建議應該選擇哪位？凱文。

Calvin: Probably the older guy from the International Trade Institute, and the woman who graduated from Tung Hai University. Her experience seems to be...
凱文：或許國貿學院年紀比較大的那位和畢業於東海大學的那位女性。她的經驗似乎……

Annie: May I interrupt? We already have many employees from Tung Hai...
安妮：我可以打個岔嗎？我們已經有許多東海畢業的員工……

Calvin: May I just finish? Her experience seems to be better than any of the other candidates. We definitely need people with experience if we are to compete with international companies.

凱文：我可以講完嗎？她的經驗似乎比其他的求職者優秀。如果我們要和國際企業競爭的話，絕對需要有經驗的人。

Betty: That's a good point.

貝蒂：這點很有道理。

Annie: I totally disagree about the woman from Tung Hai. If we are going to choose people based on experience, then we should definitely choose the woman who worked in international banking in San Francisco. What was her name? Miss Hu? None of the other candidates...

安妮：我完全不認同聘用那位畢業於東海的女性。如果我們要根據經驗來選人，那麼我們絕對應該選擇那位在舊金山國際銀行工作過的女性。她叫什麼名字來著？胡小姐嗎？其他的求職者沒有一個……

Chair: Excuse me, can I say something here? I need to tell you that Miss Hu called this morning to withdraw herself from consideration. She has already accepted a job at another company. Sorry, I forgot to tell you.

主席：對不起，這裡我可以說句話嗎？我需要告訴各位胡小姐今天早上打過電話來，表示不再考慮這個工作。她已經接受另外一家公司的工作。對不起，我忘記告訴各位了。

Betty: Oh, that's too bad.

貝蒂：喔，太可惜了。

Annie: Do you remember that guy, Bob, we hired two years ago? Remember how he always forgot his job assignments and had to be reminded? We need to be careful not to choose someone like that again. Also, he used to always...

安妮：你們記不記得我們兩年前僱用的那個家伙，鮑伯？他老是忘了自己的職務、總是需要別人提醒，你們還記得嗎？我們得小心別再選到這樣的人。而且，他以前總是……

Chair: We all remember Bob, but let's come back to the discussion of the current candidates. We need to finish this meeting soon.

主席：我們都記得鮑伯，不過讓我們回到目前人選的討論。我們需要趕緊結束這場會議。

Betty: In my view, experience is very important, so I also think the woman from Tung Hai is a good choice. Other than her, I would also agree with Calvin that the older guy from the International Trade Institute is a good candidate.

貝蒂：在我看來，經驗非常重要，所以我也認為東海那位女性是個很好的選擇。除她之外，我也同意凱文的說法，來自國貿學院年紀比較大的那個家伙是個很不錯的人選。

Chair: Annie, what do you think of that?

主席：安妮，你覺得如何？

Annie: Well, I guess experience is quite important. Since Miss Hu is off the list, I guess the woman from Tung Hai is the next best qualified. And I also see Calvin's point that it is better to have two new people who do not already know each other.

安妮：嗯，我想經驗相當重要。因為胡小姐已經不在這份名單上，我想接下來最合格的應該是東海這位女性。而且，我也認同凱文的說法，兩個新人最好彼此不認識。

Chair: It seems we agree on the two candidates. That is great, because we are almost out of time. That's all for this item. So, let's go to the closing.

主席：看起來我們已經同意要聘請這兩位新人。好極了，因為我們快要沒有時間了。這個事項的討論就告一段落。那，我們做總結吧。

Remember the Principles

各位不需要背下所有意思想同的片語或是例句。從每個主題區域選擇一個片語或是句子的範例背下來，讓它們成為你自然的風格。

You do not need to memorize all phrases or sentences that have the same meaning. Pick one phrase or sentence example from each topic area and memorize it. Let that become your natural style.

6 實戰演練 Partner Practice

依照下列情境，找個同伴一起模擬對話，作為實戰前的演練。

① A是台灣人，B是外國人。雙方都在A的公司開會。

會議的目的是討論A的產品對B的公司可能會有哪些用處。假設A有些同事也參加這次會議。

　　A：展開會議，包括介紹B

　　　　以下是會議議程。

```
議程
產品討論會議
1. 開場白
   A. 開始
   B. 歡迎
   C. 目的
   D. 預先說明
   E. 說明時間
2. 公司簡報
3. 產品簡報
4. 討論
5. 結語
```

② 這個情況很簡單，只要扮演你自己就可以了！你和你的夥伴都扮演自己的角色，為以下這些活動選些討論主題。選擇能夠讓你和夥伴輕易提出不同意見的主題。必要的時候可以改變話題，藉以維持興趣（主題舉例如下：與中國的貿易、台灣的現況、解決失業問題的方案、你們公司可以生產的新產品、你們公司可以開發的新市場等）。

1) 打岔

A：討論主題

B：討論主題

A：打岔

B：讓對方打岔（什麼都不說）

A：討論主題

B：討論主題

A：打岔

B：制止對方打岔（繼續講話）

2) 表達意見——簡短的評論

A：討論主題

B：討論主題

A：提出意見

B：評論

A：提出意見

B：表示了解

3) 表達意見——表示認同以及不認同

A：討論主題

B：討論主題

A：提供意見

B：表示認同

A：提供意見

B：表示不認同

4) 提出問題

A：討論主題

B：討論主題

A：尋求更多資訊

B：提供更多資訊

A：要求說明清楚

B：提供說明

第 **7** 章

· ·

談判
Negotiations

　　談判很刺激。做生意的核心在於成交，參與以英文進行的談判需要一些特定的字彙和特殊的用語。本章提供各位談判所需的基本英文技巧。學習好這些英文技巧，好好享受你的談判過程吧！

　　Negotiations are exciting.　Making deals is the heart of doing business.　Participating in English negotiations requires some specific vocabulary and special language functions.　This chapter provides you with the basic English skills you need.　Learn the English skills, and have a good time in your negotiations!

1 論談判　Talking about Negotiations

　　談判是會議的一種。如果能運用我們介紹的會議詞彙，你就有資格進一步學習如何進行成功的談判了。記住，談判是一種會議。所以會議所需的知識與語言技巧，在談判時都派得上用場。

　　就如同其他形式的會議，談判也有開場、過程以及結尾。談判時的開場和結尾與其他形式的會議是一樣的。在談判時必須掌握的專門英文用語，和在開會時進入主題時的用語是一樣的。以下是各位必須知道的字彙。你會在談判時用到這些字彙，討論談判事宜的時候也派得上用場。

1.1 基本字彙　Basic Vocabulary

　　請熟記這些字彙。

*BIZ*必通字彙

談判的部分 (Parts of a Negotiation Presentation)
1. proposal〔prə`pozl〕 *n.* 提案
2. offer〔`ɔfə〕 *n.* 提議；出價
3. counterproposal〔`kauntəprə,pozl〕 *n.* 對立方案
4. counteroffer〔`kauntə,ɔfə〕 *n.* 對立提議
5. position〔pə`zɪʃən〕 *n.* 立場
6. concession〔kən`sɛʃən〕 *n.* 讓步
7. condition〔kən`dɪʃən〕 *n.* 條件
8. demand〔dɪ`mænd〕 *n.* 要求

結果 (Outcomes)
1. deal〔dil〕 *n.* 交易

② agreement〔ə`grimənt〕 *n.* 協議
③ deadlock〔`dɛd‚lɑk〕 *n.* 僵局
④ resolution〔‚rɛzə`luʃən〕 *n.* 決議

談判項目 (Items to Negotiate)

① quantity〔`kwɑntətɪ〕 *n.* 數量
② style〔staɪl〕 *n.* 款式
③ shipping〔`ʃɪpɪŋ〕 *n.* 運送
④ payment terms〔`pemənt `tɜmz〕 *n.* 付款條件
⑤ discount〔`dɪskaʊnt〕 *n.* 折扣

文件 (Documents)

① contract〔`kɑntrækt〕 *n.* 合約
② papers〔`pepəz〕 *n.* 文件

實用的說法 (Useful Terms)

① estimate〔`ɛstəmɪt〕 *n.* 估價
② estimate〔`ɛstə‚met〕 *v.* 估計
③ percentage〔pə`sɛntɪdʒ〕 *n.* 百分比
④ win-win〔`wɪn`wɪn〕 *adj.* 雙贏
⑤ lose-lose〔`luz`luz〕 *adj.* 雙輸
⑥ win-lose〔`wɪn`luz〕 *adj.* 單贏

1.2 配合情境的字彙 Vocabulary in Context

　　談判用語一般來說要比其他正式場合所用的字彙艱深。談判的字彙比較偏向技術性，而且講究精準。因此，接下來的範例將幫助各位了解如何使用這些字彙。

1.2a 說明「談判部分」的字彙
'Parts of a Negotiation Presentation' Vocabulary

Show Time

❶ We would like to make our **proposal** now.
我們現在要報告我們的提案。

❷ Your **offer** is very interesting. Let's discuss it in detail.
你的提議很吸引人。我們來討論一下細節吧。

❸ Can you make a reasonable **offer** for this product?
你能否對這項產品提出合理的價錢？

❹ That finishes our proposal. Would you like to make your **counterproposal** now?
我們的提案到此告一段落。您現在要提出對立方案嗎？

❺ Your **counteroffer** is more detailed than our offer, so let's talk about that first.
你們的對立提案比我方所提的方案更詳細，所以讓我們先討論你們的提案。

❻ You know our thinking now. We would like to hear your **position**.
現在你知道我們的想法了。我們想聽聽你的立場。

❼ If you think the price is too high, we could offer a **concession**.
如果你認為價格太高，我們可以做個讓步。

❽ We can't meet your **condition**. Are you sure it cannot be changed?

你開出的條件我們無法做到。你確定不能調整一下嗎？

❾ Our **demand** in all negotiations is that trial orders must be for a minimum of 2,000 pieces.

我們在所有的談判中都要求試訂的數量至少必須達到兩千件。

◇◇◇ 小心陷阱 ◇◇◇

☹ 錯誤用法

We could offer you **concession**.

我們可以做個讓步。

☺ 正確用法

We could offer you **a concession**.

我們可以做個讓步。

1.2 b 說明「結果」的字彙 'Outcomes' Vocabulary

Show Time

❶ I don't think we can reach a **deal** unless you agree to pay five percent more.

我想我們無法做成這筆生意，除非你同意多付5％。

❷ I hope we can sign an **agreement** after this negotiation.

我希望這次協商後我們能簽署一份協議書。

❸ We seem to be in a **deadlock**. You really cannot lower the price even a little?

我們似乎陷入僵局了。你真的就沒辦法把價格稍微降低一點點嗎？

❹ I accept your **resolution**. It seems we can reach an agreement today after all!
我接受你的決議。看來我們今天還是可以達成協議。

1.2c 說明「談判項目」的字彙 'Items to Negotiate' Vocabulary

Show Time

❶ Can you offer us a **quantity** discount?
你可以給我們打個數量折扣嗎？

❷ Will you upgrade your product to a more modern **style** next season?
你們下一季能否將產品升級為較時髦的款式？

❸ **Shipping** charges are always FOB.
運費都是以船上交貨價格計算的。

❹ We accept your **payment terms**. We will pay fifty percent now and fifty percent when the order is shipped.
我們接受你的付款條件。我們現在會先付一半，出貨後再支付另外一半。

❺ If I agree to purchase more than the minimum amount, can you offer me a **discount**?
如果我同意購買超過最低標準的量，你能給我一個折扣嗎？

1.2d 說明「文件」的字彙 'Documents' Vocabulary

Show Time

❶ Can we sign the **contract** today?
我們今天可以簽約嗎？

❷ Let me ask my secretary to bring in the **papers** so you can make sure everything is okay.
讓我請秘書把文件拿進來，你可以看看是否都沒問題。

1.2e 實用的說法 Useful Terms

Show Time

❶ Please understand, this is just an **estimate** of our shipping costs.
請您了解，這只是我們對運費的估價。

❷ We **estimate** that our profit will be too low if we have to pay such a high price.
我們估計，如果我們得付這麼高的價格，利潤就太低了。

❸ The error **percentage** is too high. We really need a more effective design.
錯誤的百分比太高了。我們實在需要較有效的設計。

❹ If you place a larger order, we will give you a generous discount. It will be a **win-win** situation.
如果你們能較大量訂購，我們會給你們很大的折扣。那就會是個雙贏的局面。

❺ Maybe we should both be more flexible so that we don't end up with a **lose-lose** deal.
也許我們彼此都應該更有彈性，這樣我們的交易才不會變成雙輸。

❻ I would like to make a deal that is profitable for both of us, rather than a **win-lose** deal.
我希望做的交易對我們雙方都有利潤可言，而不是單方面獲利而已。

2 提案的談判用語
Negotiation Language for Proposals

這個單元介紹的是各位在提案時可以運用的特殊英文用語：

- 提案
- 說明價格
- 接受
- 拒絕

2.1 提案 Making a Proposal

BIZ必通句型

❶ I PROPOSE THAT...

我提議……

例 I propose that we sign a contract for a two-year deal.
我提議我們簽署一份為期兩年的合約。

例 I propose that you purchase thirty boxes of paper each month for the next twelve months.
我提議您在未來的十二個月內每個月購買三十箱紙。

❷ MY PROPOSAL IS THAT...

我的提案是……

例 My proposal is that we double our order, and you provide free shipping.
我的提案是，我們訂兩倍的量，而你提供免費運送。

❸ I SUGGEST THAT...

我建議……

例 I suggest that we agree to their payment terms.
我建議我們同意他們的付款條件。

❹ **MY SUGGESTION IS THAT...**
我的建議是……
例 My suggestion is that we reduce the payment schedule from ninety days to forty-five days.
我的建議是，我們把付款時間從九十天減少到四十五天。

❺ **WHY DON'T WE...**
我們何不……
例 Why don't we sign a contract for two hundred of your blue chairs?
我們何不簽署一份購買你們兩百張藍色椅子的合約？

❻ **WHAT ABOUT + V-ing...?**
……怎麼樣？
例 What about selling us five thousand pieces this month and ten thousand pieces next month?
這個月賣給我們五千個，下個月賣一萬個怎麼樣？
例 What about buying five hundred cans for a trial order?
試買五百罐怎麼樣？

❼ **HOW ABOUT + V-ing...?**
……如何？
例 How about offering us a ten percent discount?
提供我們百分之十的折扣如何？

❽ I THINK WE SHOULD...

我認為我們應該……

例 I think we should agree to sign a three-year contract.

我認為我們應該同意簽三年的合約。

 ◇◇◇ 小心陷阱 ◇◇◇

1 ☹ 錯誤用法

My propose is that we buy fifty units.

我提議我們購買五十套。

☺ 正確用法

I propose that we buy fifty units.

我提議我們購買五十套。

2 ☹ 錯誤用法

My suggest is that we buy fifty units.

我建議我們購買五十套。

☺ 正確用法

I suggest that we buy fifty units.

我建議我們購買五十套。

 ◇◇◇ 小心陷阱 ◇◇◇

☹ 錯誤用法

I think we should reduce **a** lead time.

我認為我們應該縮短前製時間。

☺ 正確用法

I think we should reduce **the** lead time.

我認為我們應該縮短前製時間。

Word list

lead time〔`lid `taɪm〕 *n.* 產品設計與實際生產間相隔的時間；訂貨至交貨所隔的時間

2.2 說明價格 Stating the Price

BIZ必通句型

❶ ...ARE...EACH.
……是每個……
例 They are five U.S. dollars each.
它們每個五塊美金。
例 Our CDs are twelve dollars each.
我們的 CD 每片十二美元。

❷ ...IS/ARE...PER....
……（產品）是……（單位）……（元）
例 This product is fifty U.S. cents per bottle.
這個產品每瓶是五十分美金。
例 Our candy packets are six U.S. dollars per dozen.
我們的糖果包是一打六美元。

❸ ...COST(S)...
……值……
例 It costs five hundred U.S. dollars.
這個價值五百美元。
例 The new version costs seven and a half dollars.
新的版本價值七塊半。

❹ I CAN ACCEPT... (PER...).
我可以接受（每……）……
例 I can accept twenty dollars per box.
我可以接受每盒二十元。

例 I can accept one million NT in compensation.
我可以接受新台幣一百萬元的賠償。

❺ ... (PER...) IS ACCEPTABLE.
（每……）……可以接受。
例 One hundred dollars is acceptable.
一百元可以接受。
例 Two thousand NT per piece is acceptable.
每件台幣兩千元可以接受。

2.3 接受 Accepting

BIZ必通句型

❶ THAT SOUNDS FINE.
那聽起來還不錯。

❷ THAT SOUNDS GOOD.
那聽起來蠻好的。

❸ I CAN ACCEPT THAT.
那個我可以接受。

❹ I'LL GO ALONG WITH THAT.
那個我贊同。

❺ AGREED!
同意！

❻ I AGREE TO THAT.

我同意那個。

◇◇ 小心陷阱 ◇◇

☹ 錯誤用法

I **am agree** to that.

我同意。

☺ 正確用法

I **agree** to that.

我同意。

2.4 拒絕 Declining

BIZ 必通句型

❶ I WOULD LIKE TO..., BUT...

我想要……，不過……

例 We would like to accept your offer, but it's a little too low.

我們想要接受你提的價格，不過有點太低了。

❷ I WISH I COULD..., BUT...

但願我能……，不過……

例 I wish we could offer free shipping, but we cannot afford it at this time.

但願我們能提供免費運送，不過我們這時候負擔不起。

❸ I WOULD BE HAPPY TO..., BUT...

我很樂意……，不過……

> 例 I would be happy to increase the size of the order, but we cannot sell the items so quickly.
> 我很樂意增加訂單的規模，不過我們無法這麼快賣掉這些物品。

❹ I AM SORRY TO SAY WE CAN'T...

我很抱歉地說，我們無法……

> 例 I am sorry to say we can't lower the price so much.
> 我很抱歉地說，我們無法把價格降這麼多。

❺ I REGRET TO SAY...

我很遺憾地說……

> 例 I regret to say your offer is just a little too high.
> 我很遺憾地說，你提的價格實在有點太高了。

❻ THAT'S JUST NOT POSSIBLE.

那實在不可能。

❼ THAT'S OUT OF THE QUESTION.

那根本不可能。

(Show Time)

❶ Negotiator for Company A: Well, shall we start the negotiation?

Negotiator for Company B: Sure. Why don't you tell me the price you would like to sell your paint at?

Word list

out of the question〔`aut əv ðə `kwɛstʃən〕adj. 決不可能的

Negotiator for Company A: Our house paint is three U.S. dollars per can.

Negotiator for Company B: Then I propose that my company buy 1,500 cans.

Negotiator for Company A: I would be happy to sell you 1,500 cans, but we usually agree to minimum orders of 2,000 cans.

Negotiator for Company B: Let me think. If I purchase 2,000 cans, how about lowering the price?

Negotiator for Company A: I can accept U.S. 2.80 per can.

Negotiator for Company B: That sounds fine. Then I will purchase 2,000 cans.

A公司的談判代表：嗯，我們可以開始談判了嗎？

B公司的談判代表：當然。何不告訴我你們打算以什麼價格出售你們的油漆？

A公司的談判代表：我們公司的家用油漆每罐三美元。

B公司的談判代表：那我提議我們公司購買一千五百罐。

A公司的談判代表：我很樂意賣給你們一千五百罐，不過通常我們的最低訂貨量為兩千罐。

B公司的談判代表：讓我想想看。如果我購買兩千罐，能不能降低售價？

A公司的談判代表：我可以接受每罐美金兩塊八的價格。

B公司的談判代表：聽起來不錯。那我就買兩千罐。

❷ Negotiator for Company A: Why don't we sign a contract for a one-year deal?

Negotiator for Company B: That sounds good, but it depends on the price of your product.

Negotiator for Company A: How about twenty U.S. dollars per box?

Negotiator for Company B: I regret to say we can't pay more than eighteen dollars per box.

Negotiator for Company A: And how many boxes do you need per month?

Negotiator for Company B: Five hundred.

Negotiator for Company A: I'll go along with that.

A公司的談判代表：我們何不簽署為期一年期的合約？

B公司的談判代表：聽起來不錯，不過這要看你們產品的售價。

A公司的談判代表：每盒二十美元怎麼樣？

B公司的談判代表：我很遺憾地說，我們無法支付每盒十八美元以上的價格。

A公司的談判代表：你們每個月需要幾盒？

B公司的談判代表：五百盒。

A公司的談判代表：我同意。

3 特殊情況的談判用語
Negotiation Language for Special Situations

這個部分介紹談判過程常見的特定英文用語。

- 詢問意見
- 說明狀況
- 釐清
- 禮貌地提出建議
- 談判成敗的表達方法

3.1 詢問意見 Asking for Opinions

BIZ 必通句型

❶ WHAT DO YOU THINK ABOUT...?

你覺得……如何？

例 What do you think about our offer?

你覺得我們的提議如何？

❷ I WOULD LIKE TO HEAR YOUR OPINION ABOUT...

我想要聽聽你對……的意見。

例 I would like to hear your opinion about our new product.

我想要聽聽你對我們新產品的意見。

❸ I AM CURIOUS TO HEAR YOUR OPINION ABOUT...

我很好奇，想聽聽你對……的意見。

例 I am curious to hear your opinion about the second part of our offer.

我很好奇，想聽聽你對我們提議第二個部分的意見。

❹ COULD YOU GIVE ME YOUR OPINION?
您能不能告訴我您的意見？

❺ WHAT'S YOUR OPINION?
你有什麼意見？

❻ WHAT IS YOUR REACTION TO THAT?
你對那有什麼回應？

❼ WHAT IS YOUR VIEW?
你有什麼看法？

◇◇◇ 小心陷阱 ◇◇◇

☹ 錯誤用法

How do you think about our products?
你覺得我們的產品怎麼樣？

☺ 正確用法

What do you think about our products?
你覺得我們的產品怎麼樣？

Show Time

❶ A: That concludes item three of our proposal. What do you think about our proposal?

B: Well, it is very interesting. But I would like to offer a counterproposal.

A：那總結了我們提案的第三項。你對我們的提案有什麼看法？

B：嗯，很有意思。但是我想要提出一個對立方案。

❷ A: We think the older version of your office fan is actually better for the small business market. Could you give me your opinion?

B: Sure. I think the new model is actually better for small business...

A：我們認為你們舊款的辦公室風扇其實比較適合小公司的市場。您能不能告訴我您的意見？

B：當然。我認為新款其實比較適合小公司……

3.2 說明狀況 Stating Conditions

BIZ 必通句型

❶ IF YOU..., I WILL...

如果你……，我將會……

例 If you reduce the price by five percent, I will increase our order to 750 units.

如果你減少價格百分之五，我會增加我們的訂貨量到七百五十套。

❷ I WILL..., IF YOU...

我會……，如果你……

例 I will customize your order, if you order more than 3,000 pieces.

如果您的訂貨量超過三千個，我會依您個別的要求特別製作。

Word list

customize〔`kʌstəmˌaɪz〕 v. 定製；定做

❸ IF YOU COULD/WOULD..., I COULD/WOULD...

如果您可以 / 願意……，我可以 / 願意……

例 If you would customize the product for us, I could accept the deal.

如果你們願為我們特別製作產品，我可以接受這筆交易。

例 If you could ship the products for free, I would like to accept your overall proposal.

如果你們可以免費運送產品，我願意接受你們的整體提案。

例 If you could lower the shipping cost, I could place a larger order.

如果你們可以降低運費，我就可以訂更多。

❹ I COULD/WOULD..., IF YOU COULD/WOULD...

我可以 / 願意……，如果你可以 / 願意……

（以下範例只是把句型 3 的例句倒過來講而已）

例 I could accept the deal, if you would customize the product for us.

例 I would like to accept your overall proposal, if you could ship the products for free.

例 I could place a larger order, if you could lower the shipping cost.

❺ I CAN..., IF YOU...

我可以……，如果你……

例 I can offer a significant discount, if you sign a long-term contract.

如果你簽訂長期合約的話，我可以提供很大的折扣。

◇◇◇ 小心陷阱 ◇◇◇

☹ 錯誤用法

If you would lower the price, I **could like** to purchase more.

如果你願意降價，我就會買更多。

☺ 正確用法

If you would lower the price, I **would like** to purchase more.

如果你願意降價，我就會買更多。

Show Time

❶ A: We can offer you a price of two U.S. dollars per can.

B: If you could reduce the price to 1.80, we could purchase an extra 10,000 cans.

A：我們可以提供每罐兩美元的價格。

B：如果你可以降價到一塊八，我們可以多訂一萬罐。

❷ A: So, you would like to order 500 speaker units.

B: Yes. And if you provide free shipping, I will also place an order for your speaker covers.

A：那，你想要訂五百組擴音喇叭。

B：是的，而且如果你們提供免費運貨，我也會訂購你們擴音喇叭的蓋子。

3.3 釐清 Clarifying

BIZ必通句型

❶ LET'S GO OVER...AGAIN.
讓我們重新再看一遍……
例 Let's go over that again.
讓我們重新把那再看一遍。
例 Let's go over the cost comparison again.
讓我們重新看一遍成本比較。

❷ CAN YOU GO OVER...AGAIN?
你可以重新講一遍……嗎？
例 Can you go over your pricing system again?
你可以重新講一遍你們的定價機制嗎？

❸ I WANT TO MAKE...CLEAR.
我想要把……說清楚。
例 I want to make our point clear. What we mean is...
我想要把我們的重點說清楚。我們的意思是……
例 I want to make the offer clear, so let me repeat it.
我想要把提案說清楚，所以讓我再講一遍。

❹ I'M NOT CLEAR ON...
我對……不清楚。
例 I'm not clear on your point. Could you say that again?
你的論點我並不清楚。你可以再說一遍嗎？

❺ COULD YOU CLARIFY...?
您可以說明……嗎？

例 Could you clarify point two of your offer?
您可以把提案當中的第二個點說明清楚嗎？

⑥ COULD YOU BE MORE SPECIFIC?
您可以說得更詳細一些嗎？

⑦ I THINK YOU ARE SAYING... IS THAT RIGHT?
我想你說的是……，對不對？
例 I think you are saying the new models are a little too expensive for your budget. Is that right?
我想你說的是新款產品對你們的預算而言有點太貴了，對不對？

Show Time

❶ A: I don't quite understand the shipping procedures.
B: Okay, let's go over that again.

- -

A：我不是很清楚運貨的程序。
B：好，讓我們重新再看一遍。

❷ A: That is our suggestion for a customized version of the knives.
B: I'm not clear on the exact appearance of the customized version. Can you explain it again or show us a picture of it?

- -

A：這是我們對特製刀具款式的建議。
B：我對特製款式的實際外觀不是很清楚。你可以再解說一遍或是給我們看看照片？

3.4 提出禮貌的建議 Making Polite Suggestions

BIZ 必通句型

❶ WOULD YOU BE WILLING TO...?

你願意……嗎？

例 Would you be willing to increase the size of your order?

你願意增加你訂單的規模嗎？

❷ PERHAPS YOU COULD...

或許你可以……

例 Perhaps you could offer us a wider variety of colors.

或許你可以提供我們更多種的顏色。

❸ COULD YOU...?

你可以……嗎？

例 Could you upgrade to the newer version?

你們可以升級到比較新的版本嗎？

❹ IS IT POSSIBLE TO...?

有沒有……的可能？

例 Is it possible to customize the order?

訂貨有沒有可能依我們的需要特別製造？

❺ I WOULD APPRECIATE IT IF YOU COULD...

如果你可以……，我會很感激。

例 I would appreciate it if you could lower the transportation cost a little.

如果你們可以把運費降低一點，我會很感激。

⑥ HOW ABOUT + V-ing?

……如何？

例 How about increasing the size of your order?

增加你們訂單的規模如何？

⑦ WHAT ABOUT + V-ing?

……怎麼樣？

例 What about delaying your order for a few weeks?

把你們訂的貨延後幾個禮拜怎麼樣？

 ◇◇◇ 小心陷阱 ◇◇◇

☹ 錯誤用法

I'd **appreciate** if you would lower the price.

如果你們能降低價錢，我會很感激。

☺ 正確用法

I'd **appreciate it** if you would lower the price.

如果你們能降低價錢，我會很感激。

Show Time

❶ A: Our coconut soap costs one dollar and twenty cents U.S. per bar. They are shipped in crates—1,000 per crate.

B: That is a little more than we thought they might cost. Would you be willing to provide free shipping to Los Angeles?

A：我們的椰子肥皂每個美金一塊，是以條板箱裝運——每個條板箱裝一千個。

B：價錢有點超出我們原本的預期。你們願意免費運到洛杉磯嗎？

❷ A: We would like to have ninety-day net payment terms, if possible.

B: Perhaps you could accept sixty-day net payment terms.

A：如果可能的話，我們想採九十天期的付款方式。

B：或許你可以接受六十天期的付款方式。

❸ A: Could you increase your order to 25,000 pieces?

B: I would like to, but my company cannot afford more than 15,000 at this time.

A：你可以增加訂貨量到兩萬五千個嗎？

B：我很樂意，不過我們公司這時候無法負擔一萬五千個以上。

❹ A: We suggest that you ship half the order now and the other half in two months.

B: I wish we could, but we cannot produce the final quantity until three months later.

A：我們建議你現在運一半的貨，兩個月後再運另外一半。

B：但願我們可以，不過最後的量我們要等到三個月後才能生產出來。

3.5 談判成敗的表達方法 Expressing Success or Failure

詢問交易成功與否的方式如下：

"Is it a deal?"

「成交了嗎？」

"Do we have a deal?"
「我們成交了嗎？」

下列的句型則是回答上述問句的方式：

BIZ必通句型

❶ **DEAL!**
成交！

❷ **IT'S A DEAL!**
成交！

❸ **WE HAVE A DEAL!**
我們成交！

❹ **LET'S DO IT!**
我們就這麼做吧！

❺ **SORRY, NO DEAL.**
對不起，不成。

❻ **I'M AFRAID NOT.**
恐怕不行。

Show Time

❶ A: Is it a deal?
　 B: It's a deal.

　 A：成交了嗎？
　 B：成交。

❷ A: Is it a deal?

B: I'm sorry. No deal. Let's discuss the style change a little more.

A：成交了嗎？

B：很抱歉。不成。我們再多討論一下風格的調整。

4 委婉的說法 Downtoning

「Downtoning」的意思是用比較委婉的方法來傳達壞消息。美語的表達很直接、而且清晰，不過這並不表示就不顧及其他人的感受。說話的人透過委婉的說法，可以顧及聽者的感受，也有助於維繫雙方和諧的關係。

BIZ必通句型

❶ I AM AFRAID...
我恐怕……

例 I am afraid we cannot ship the products in time.
我恐怕我們無法準時運送這批產品。

例 The meeting will have to be postponed, I am afraid.
會議恐怕得延後了。

例 I am afraid we don't have a deal.
恐怕我們並沒有成交。

❷ ...A LITTLE/A BIT/JUST...
……有點……

例 The presentation will be a little late.
簡報將會晚一些舉行。

例 That price is a bit too high.
那個價格有點太貴了。

例 The shipping cost is just ten percent more than we expected.
船運的成本只比我們原先預期的多出百分之十。

❸ PERHAPS...

或許……

例 Perhaps that price is too high.

或許那個價格太貴了。

例 Perhaps we can ship the products a week later.

或許我們可以晚一個禮拜再把貨物運送出去。

以上這些委婉的說法可以綜合使用。

Show Time

❶ I am afraid that is a little bit too expensive.

恐怕那有點太貴了。

❷ That will take one week longer than expected, I am afraid.

恐怕那會比預期的多花一個禮拜時間。

❸ Perhaps that lead time is a little too slow.

或許那個前製時間有點太慢了。

5 談判範例 Example Negotiation

Show Time

Ms. Kuo : You can see that my company's travel books are high quality. What's your opinion?

Mr. Jackson : Yes, they are pretty good. I think they will sell well in our west coast bookstores. Let me make you an offer. I think we should agree to a quantity of two thousand books for each of the major East Asian countries.

Ms. Kuo : Alright. As you know, we have books for seven countries, so that would be fourteen thousand books total.

Mr. Jackson : What is the price you charge for fourteen thousand books?

Ms. Kuo : Travel books are two dollars and forty cents, U.S. So, fourteen thousand books would be thirty-three thousand six hundred dollars.

Mr. Jackson : If you could provide a discount, I could consider ordering some of your regional maps.

Ms. Kuo : How many maps are you thinking about?

Mr. Jackson : Maybe about two hundred.

Ms. Kuo : Perhaps you could order five hundred.

Mr. Jackson : I'll go along with that.

Ms. Kuo : I want to make that clear. You will order fourteen thousand books and five hundred maps, if I offer a discount on the books.

Mr. Jackson : That's right, if the discount is enough.

Ms. Kuo : What about a five percent discount?

Mr. Jackson : I'm afraid that is not what I had in mind. How about a ten percent discount?

Ms. Kuo : I wish I could, but a ten percent discount is just too much on an order of fourteen thousand books. I suggest that we go for a seven percent discount. What do you think about a seven percent discount?

Mr. Jackson : Agreed!

Ms. Kuo : Good. Then, is it a deal?

Mr. Jackson : It's a deal!

郭女士 ：你可以看到我們公司的旅遊書籍品質很好。你有什麼意見？

傑克森先生：是的，它們相當好。我認為它們在我們西岸的書店會賣得相當好。我給你一個提議。我想我們應該可以同意每個主要東亞國家的書各兩千本的量。

郭女士 ：好的。誠如您所知，我們有介紹東亞的七個國家的書，那就是總共一萬四千本。

傑克森先生：一萬四千本書你要開多少價錢？

郭女士 ：旅遊書是美金兩塊四。所以，一萬四千本就是三萬三千六百美元。

傑克森先生：如果你可以提供折扣，我可以考慮訂一些你們的區域地圖。

郭女士 ：你考慮訂多少地圖？

傑克森先生：大約兩百幅吧。

郭女士 ：或許你可以訂個五百幅。

傑克森先生：我同意。

郭女士　　：我要弄清楚。如果我書打折的話，你就會訂購一萬四千本書和五百份地圖。

傑克森先生：對的，如果折扣夠的話。

郭女士　　：95折怎麼樣？

傑克森先生：恐怕和我心裡所想的有些差距。打9折如何？

郭女士　　：但願可以，不過百分之十的折扣對於一萬四千本書的訂量來說有點太多了。我建議少個百分之七。你覺得百分之七的折扣怎麼樣？

傑克森先生：同意！

郭女士　　：好的，那麼，成交了嗎？

傑克森先生：成交！

Remember the Principles

1 談判是會議的一種。當你參與談判時，記住開會用的英文技巧。

A negotiation is one kind of meeting. Remember your meeting-English skills when you participate in a negotiation.

2 談判英文用語比其他正式的英文用語更要講究精準。所以，對字彙以及片語的用法應該特別地注意。

Negotiation English is more sophisticated than other kinds of formal English. So, pay careful attention to the way vocabulary and phrases are used.

6 實戰演練 Partner Practice

依據下列情境，找個同伴一起模擬對話，作爲實戰前的演練。

1 A是台灣人。B是到A公司拜訪的外國人。B想要購買A的產品。雙方對這筆交易進行談判。

1) B：詢價

　　A：報價

2) B：提案，詢問意見

　　A：給予意見

3) B：提案

　　A：說明條件

4) B：提案

　　A：提出對立方案

　　B：釐清提案

5) B：提案

　　A：禮貌地提出建議

　　B：禮貌地拒絕這個建議

第 **8** 章

介紹自己的公司
Presenting Your Company

　　當外國人來到台灣和你談生意，你可能想要帶領對方參觀你的公司。本章將會提供各位在這種提供資訊、有趣的參觀行程當中所需的英文用語。此處提供的部分英文用語在會議、電話或是簡報中談到你的公司時也非常有用。所以，本章介紹的英文用語用途相當廣泛。

When a foreigner comes to Taiwan to discuss business with you, you will probably want to give a tour of your company. This chapter provides the English you need to give an informative and interesting tour. Some of the English presented here is also very useful for talking about your company in a meeting, over the phone, or in a presentation. So, the English in this chapter is broadly useful.

1 介紹公司的字彙
Vocabulary for Introducing the Company

BIZ 必通字彙

基本資訊 (Basic Information)
❶ found〔faʊnd〕 v. 成立
❷ sales volume〔`selz ˏvɑljəm〕 n. 銷售量
❸ brand〔brænd〕 n. 品牌
❹ trademark〔`tredˏmɑrk〕 n. 商標
❺ vendor〔`vɛndɚ〕 n. 賣方；小販
❻ market〔`mɑrkɪt〕 n. 市場
❼ distribute〔dɪs`trɪbjut〕 v. 分發；供應（貨物）
❽ staff〔stæf〕 n. 人員
❾ retail〔`ritel〕 n. 零售
❿ wholesale〔`holˏsel〕 n. 批發

公司各部分 (Parts of the Company)
❶ showroom〔`joˏrum〕 n. 展示室
❷ conference room〔`kɑnfərəns ˏrum〕 n. 會議室
❸ office complex〔`ɔfɪs `kɑmplɛks〕 n. 綜合辦公大樓
❹ warehouse〔`wɛrˏhaʊs〕 n. 倉庫

公司特質 (Company Qualities)
❶ innovative〔`ɪnəˏvetɪv〕 adj. 創新的
❷ revolutionary〔ˏrɛvə`luʃənˏɛrɪ〕 adj. 革命性的
❸ progressive〔prə`grɛsɪv〕 adj. 進步的

關鍵的動詞 (Key Verbs)
❶ export〔ɪks`port〕 v. 出口

❷ import 〔ɪm`port〕 *v.* 進口
❸ source 〔sors〕 *v.* 向⋯⋯採購
❹ expand 〔ɪk`spænd〕 *v.* 擴張
❺ relocate 〔ri`loket〕 *v.* 搬遷

公司的種類 (Kinds of Companies)
❶ retailer 〔`ritelɚ〕 *n.* 零售商
❷ wholesaler 〔`hol,selɚ〕 *n.* 大盤商
❸ middleman 〔`mɪdḷ,mæn〕 *n.* 中介商
❹ distributor 〔dɪ`strɪbjʊtɚ〕 *n.* 經銷商；批發商

1.1 說明「基本資訊」的字彙
'Basic Information' Language

Show Time

❶ Our company was founded in 1996.
我們公司成立於一九九六年。

❷ We have a sales volume of 20,000 cases per month.
我們每個月的銷售量達兩萬箱。

❸ Our brand of powdered drinks is similar to Kool-Aid in the U.S.
我們粉狀飲料的品牌和美國的 Kool-Aid 類似。

❹ Our trademark consists of our company name with a rainbow above it.
我們的商標包括我們公司的名稱及其上方的彩虹圖案。

❺ A **vendor** in South Africa supplies us with the metal rods we need to make our products.
一家南非廠商提供我們生產所需的金屬棒。

❻ The **market** is responding very favorably to our products.
市場對我們的產品反應相當不錯。

❼ We **distribute** shoes made in China to stores around the island.
我們批發中國製鞋子給本島各地的商店。

❽ We have a **staff** of more than 100 people.
我們的員工超過一百人。

❾ We sell our products to **retail** stores in Taiwan and Japan.
我們銷售產品到台灣以及日本的零售店。

❿ Our company is a **wholesale** supply company.
我們公司是個大盤的供應商。

◇◇◇ 小心陷阱 ◇◇◇

☹ 錯誤用法
Our company was **found** ten years ago.
我們公司是十年前創立的。

☺ 正確用法
Our company was **founded** ten years ago.
我們公司是十年前創立的。

1.2 說明「公司各部分」的字彙
'Parts of the Company' Language

Show Time

❶ Here is the **showroom**, where we display our imported Italian models.
這兒是展示室，我們在此展示公司進口的義大利機型。

❷ Let's go to the **conference room** to begin our meeting.
我們到會議室開始我們的會議。

❸ Thirty people work in our **office complex** on the third floor.
我們的綜合辦公大樓三樓有三十個人在工作。

❹ Our **warehouse** is on the south side of the city.
我們的倉庫位於市區的南邊。

1.3 說明「公司特質」的字彙
'Company Qualities' Language

Show Time

❶ Our company is very **innovative**.
我們公司非常有創新力。

❷ We used titanium when other companies were still using aluminum. This makes our company **revolutionary**.
當別家公司還在用鋁的時候，我們就已經在用鈦的材質了。這讓我們公司具革命性。

❸ We are a **progressive** company, changing our products every year to keep up with consumer style popularity.
我們是一家先進的公司，每年都會調整我們的產品，以跟上消費風格的流行。

◇◇◇ 小心陷阱 ◇◇◇

☹ 錯誤用法
Our company is very **innovation**.
我們公司很有創新的精神。

☺ 正確用法
Our company is very **innovative**.
我們公司很有創新的精神。

1.4 說明「關鍵動詞」的用語 'Key Verbs' Language

Show Time

❶ We **export** our products to New Zealand and Australia.
我們出口我們的產品到紐西蘭和澳洲。

Word list

titanium〔taɪˋtenɪəm〕 *n.* 鈦

② We **import** our fabric from India.
我們從印度進口我們的布料。

③ We **source** our materials from countries in Southeast Asia.
我們原料來自東南亞國家。

④ Next year we will **expand** our facilities in Kaohsiung.
明年我們將擴大高雄的廠房。

⑤ In a few years we hope to **relocate** to southern China.
幾年後我們希望遷到中國南部。

1.5 說明「公司種類」的用語
'Kinds of Companies' Language

Show Time

❶ We are a fashion clothing **retailer**.
我們是流行服飾的零售商。

❷ We are a music CD **wholesaler**.
我們是音樂CD批發商。

❸ We are the **middleman** for a plastics company in Malaysia.
我們是馬來西亞一家塑膠公司的中間商。

❹ We are the **distributor** for a cleaning supplies company in the U.S. We sell their products to stores in Taiwan.

我們是美國一家清潔用品公司的經銷商。我們把他們的產品賣給台灣的商店。

◇◇◇ 小心陷阱 ◇◇◇

☹ 錯誤用法

Is your company **distribution**?

你們公司是經銷商嗎？

☺ 正確用法

Is your company **a distributor**?

你們公司是經銷商嗎？

2 帶領訪客參觀公司 Giving a Tour

2.1 指引 Guiding

*BIZ*必通句型

❶ FOLLOW ME.

請跟我來。

例 Please follow me this way.

請跟著我這邊走。

例 Follow me to the guest room.

請跟我到會客室。

❷ LET ME SHOW YOU...

讓我向您展示……

例 Let me show you our printing center.

讓我向您展示我們的印製中心。

❸ HAVE YOU SEEN...?

您有沒有看過……？

例 Have you seen our laboratory?

您有沒有看過我們的實驗室？

❹ LET'S TAKE A LOOK AT...

讓我們看看……

例 Let's take a look at the video conference room.

讓我們看看視訊會議室。

❺ WOULD YOU LIKE TO SEE...?

您要不要看看……？

例 Would you like to see our product displays?

您要不要看看我們的產品產示？

❻ WHAT WOULD YOU LIKE TO SEE NEXT?

您接下來想看些什麼？

❼ SHALL WE TAKE A LOOK AT...?

我們看看……好嗎？

例 Shall we take a look at the computing center?

我們看看電腦中心好嗎？

◇◇◇ 小心陷阱 ◇◇◇

☹ 錯誤用法

Have you **been seen** our computer room?

您有沒有參觀過我們的電腦中心？

☺ 正確用法

Have you **seen** our computer room?

您有沒有參觀過我們的電腦中心？

2.2 說明方向 Directing

BIZ必通句型

❶ GO ALONG...

請沿著……走。

例 Please go along that hallway. You will see the meeting room on the right side.

請沿著那個走廊走。您會看到會議室在您右手邊。

❷ **TURN... (DIRECTION)... (PREPOSITION) THE... (PLACE).**

在……（地方）……（方向）轉

例 Turn left at the cafeteria.

在自助餐廳左轉。

例 Turn right before the stairs.

在樓梯之前右轉。

例 Turn left after the large door.

過那扇大門後左轉。

❸ **TAKE THE...TO THE...**

搭……到……

例 Take the elevator to the fifth floor.

搭乘電梯到五樓。

例 Take the stairs to the second floor.

走樓梯到二樓。

❹ **WHEN YOU COME TO THE..., ...**

當你到……時，……

例 When you come to the stairs, go up.

當你碰到樓梯時，就上樓。

例 When you come to the restroom, turn right.

當你走到洗手間時，右轉。

❺ WHEN YOU GET TO THE..., ...

當你到……時，……

例 When you get to the conference room, go inside.

當你到了會議室時，走進去。

❻ GO...UNTIL YOU...

走……直到……

例 Go straight until you reach the stairs.

一直往前走到樓梯處。

例 Go down until you see the main desk.

往下走直到你看到大廳櫃檯為止。

◇◇◇ 小心陷阱 ◇◇◇

☹ 錯誤用法

When you **coming** to the front desk, turn left.

當你到了櫃檯，左轉。

☺ 正確用法

When you **come** to the front desk, turn left.

當你到了櫃檯，左轉。

2.3 說明地點 Locating

BIZ必通句型

❶ ...IS ON THE...

……在……邊。

例 The manager's office is on the right.

經理的辦公室在右邊。

例 The water fountain is on the left side of the room.
飲水機在房間的左邊。

❷ ...IS TO...

……在……邊。

例 The restroom is to your left.
洗手間在您的左手邊。

例 The computer printer is to your right.
印表機在您的右手邊。

❸ ...IS NEXT TO THE...

……在……旁邊。

例 The supervisor's office is next to the general manager's office.
主管辦公室在總經理辦公室的旁邊。

例 The computer printer is next to the secretary's desk.
印表機在秘書辦公桌的旁邊。

❹ ...IS ON THE OTHER SIDE OF THE...

……在……的另一邊。

例 The factory is on the other side of the city.
工廠在市區的另一邊。

例 The guest lounge is on the other side of the building.
來賓休息室在大樓的另外一邊。

例 The President's office is on the other side of this wall.
總裁辦公室在這面牆的那一邊。

⑤ ...JUST...

……就在……

例 The room is just to your right.

這房間就在您的右手邊。

例 The office is just a little further ahead.

辦公室就在前面一點。

例 The copy machine is just around the corner.

影印機就在轉角那邊。

3 說明產品的字彙
Vocabulary for Talking about Products

BIZ必通字彙

原料 (Materials)

❶ alloy〔`ælɔɪ〕 *n.* 合金

❷ raw material〔`rɔ mə`tɪrɪəl〕 *n.* 原物料

❸ be made of *v.* 以……製成

產品品質 (Product Qualities)

❶ state of the art〔`stet əv ðə `ɑrt〕 *adj.* 尖端科技

❷ cutting edge〔`kʌtɪŋ `ɛdʒ〕 *n.* 先鋒地位

❸ hi-tech〔`haɪ `tɛk〕 *adj.* 高科技的

❹ durable〔`djʊrəbl〕 *adj.* 耐用的

❺ long-lasting〔`lɔŋ `læstɪŋ〕 *adj.* 持久的

❻ economical〔,ikə`nɑmɪkl〕 *adj.* 經濟的

❼ extensive〔ɪk`stɛnsɪv〕 *adj.* 廣泛的

❽ defect ratio〔`difɛkt `reʃo〕 *n.* 瑕疵率

❾ product life〔`prɑdəkt ,laɪf〕 *n.* 產品壽命

關鍵動詞 (Key Verbs)

❶ loosen〔`lusn̩〕 *v.* 放鬆　　❷ tighten〔`taɪtn̩〕 *v.* 縮緊

❸ fasten〔`fæsn̩〕 *v.* 繫牢　　❹ unfasten〔ʌn`fæsn̩〕 *v.* 解開

❺ launch〔lɔntʃ〕 *v.* 推出（也可當名詞用）

❻ plug〔plʌg〕 *v.* 插上插頭

❼ unplug〔,ʌn`plʌg〕 *v.* 拔掉插頭

❽ screw on〔`skru `ɑn〕 *v.* 旋緊

❾ screw off〔`skru `ɔf〕 *v.* 旋轉開

❿ unscrew〔ʌn`sku〕 *v.* 打開

廣告文宣 (Printed Materials)

❶ flyer〔`flaɪɚ〕 *n.* 傳單

❷ brochure〔bro`ʃʊr〕 *n.* 小冊子

❸ catalog〔`kætəlɔg〕 *n.* 目錄　❹ booklet〔`bʊklɪt〕 *n.* 小冊子

❺ pamphlet〔`pæmflɪt〕 *n.* 小冊子

❻ manual〔`mænjʊəl〕 *n.* 手冊

示範用語（動詞……名詞）[Demonstration Terms (verb...noun)]

❶ push/press...button〔pʊʃ〕/〔prɛs〕...〔`bʌtn̩〕按／壓……按鈕

❷ turn...knob〔tɜn〕...〔nɑb〕轉……把手

❸ turn...handle〔tɜn〕...〔`hændl̩〕轉……把手

❹ grab...handle〔græb〕...〔`hændl̩〕握著……把手

❺ grasp...handle〔græsp〕...〔`hændl̩〕抓著……把手

❻ flick...switch〔flɪk〕...〔swɪtʃ〕輕彈……開關

❼ insert...plug〔ɪn`sɜt〕...〔plʌg〕插入……插頭

❽ plug...plug in/into〔plʌg〕...〔plʌg〕〔ɪn〕/〔`ɪntu〕插入……插頭

❾ unplug...plug〔ʌn`plʌg〕...〔plʌg〕拔開……插頭

❿ lock...lock〔lɑk〕...〔lɑk〕鎖上……鎖

⓫ unlock...lock〔ʌn`lɑk〕...〔lɑk〕打開……鎖

⓬ snap...snap〔snæp〕...〔snæp〕按下……按扣

⓭ button...button〔`bʌtn̩〕...〔`bʌtn̩〕扣上……鈕扣

產品總類 (Varieties of Products)

❶ selection〔sə`lɛkʃən〕 *n.* 挑選；精選

❷ line〔laɪn〕 *n.* 款式

❸ version〔`vɜʒən〕 *n.* 版；樣式

❹ range〔rendʒ〕 *n.* 範圍　❺ style〔staɪl〕 *n.* 款式；風格

❻ model〔`mɑdl̩〕 *n.* 模式；型號

❼ design〔dɪ`zaɪn〕 *n.* 設計

雜項 (Miscellaneous)
❶ be made by *v.* 用⋯⋯製造
❷ demonstration〔͵dɛmən`streʃən〕*n.* 示範
❸ shortage〔`ʃɔrtɪdʒ〕*n.* 短缺
❹ surplus〔`sɝpləs〕*n.* 多餘（的量）
❺ order〔`ɔrdɚ〕*n.* 訂貨；訂單

3.1 說明「原料」的用語 'Materials' Language

Show Time

❶ The metal in our products is an **alloy** that is very strong and flexible.
我們產品中的金屬是相當強勁而且有彈性的合金。

❷ Most of our **raw materials** come from Indonesia.
我們多數的原料都是從印尼進口的。

❸ The frames of our clocks are **made of** wood, not plastic.
我們時鐘的外框是木製的，不是塑膠的。

 ◇◇ 小心陷阱 ◇◇

☹ 錯誤用法
This product is **made by** plastic.
這個產品是塑膠製成的。
☺ 正確用法
This product is **made of** plastic.
這個產品是塑膠製成的。

3.2 說明「產品品質」的用語 'Product Qualities' Language

Show Time

❶ Our calculators use **state-of-the-art** technology.
我們計算機使用的是尖端科技。

❷ This product is on the **cutting edge** of radio technology.
這個產品是最先進的無線電技術。

❸ Our **hi-tech** coffee makers grind the beans, pour in the water automatically, and make the coffee for you.
我們高科技的咖啡機能研磨咖啡豆、自動注水,並能為為你煮好咖啡。

❹ See how **durable** our luggage is. You can throw it around, and it doesn't even scratch.
看看我們的行李箱有多麼的耐用。你可以到處摔看看,行李箱上頭連點刮痕都沒有。

❺ Our toothbrushes are **long-lasting**. The quality remains high for three months of usage.
我們的牙刷很持久耐用。使用三個月後的品質還是很好。

❻ Our radios are very **economical**. They use little battery power, so you can save a lot of money on batteries.
我們的收音機非常經濟。他們所耗的電池電量很低,所以你可以節省很多電池的錢。

❼ The ways you can use our soap are **extensive**. You can clean anything in your house, including your clothes. You can even clean your car.

我們肥皂的用途很廣。你可以用來清潔屋子裡頭任何東西,包括你的衣服。你甚至可以用來清洗你的車子。

❽ The **defect ratio** of our crystal dolls is only 1.5 percent.

我們水晶娃娃的瑕疵率只有百分之一點五。

❾ The **product life** of our microwave ovens is more than ten years.

我們微波爐的產品生命週期超過十年。

◇◇◇ 小心陷阱 ◇◇◇

☹ 錯誤用法

Our **production** has a product life of five years.

我們產品的產品壽命是五年。

☺ 正確用法

Our **product** has a product life of five years.

我們產品的產品壽命是五年。

3.3 關鍵性的動詞 'Key Verbs' Language

Show Time

❶ If the hat is too tight, you can easily **loosen** it.

如果這個帽子太緊,你可以輕易地把它放鬆。

❷ You can **tighten** our bicycle brakes with just your fingers!
你只要用手指就可以上緊我們腳踏車的煞車。

❸ This high-quality leather strap easily **fastens** on to any of our bags.
這個高品質的皮帶可以輕易地繫牢我們的任何袋子。

❹ You can **unfasten** the cover by pulling here.
你只要拉這裡就可以打開封蓋。

❺ We will **launch** our new cooking products next spring.
我們將於明年春季推出我們新的烹飪用品。

❻ Our computer components are easy to install. Just **plug** them into any computer.
我們的電腦零件很容易安裝。只要把它們插在任何電腦上即可。

❼ If the metal gets too hot, you can **unplug** the machine.
如果金屬變得很熱,你可以把機器的插頭拔掉。

❽ It is easy to **screw on** the lid.
蓋子很容易轉上。

❾ You can easily **screw** this part **off**.
你可以很輕易地轉下這個零件。

❿ You can **unscrew** the cover whenever you want.
你可以隨時把蓋子轉下來。

3.4 說明廣告文宣的用語 'Printed Materials' Language

Show Time

❶ We hire students to give away these **flyers** in the downtown area.
我們雇請學生在市中心發這些傳單。

❷ This four-page **brochure** shows our most popular models.
這份四頁的小冊子展示我們最受歡迎的機型。

❸ You can take a look at our **catalog**. It contains every product we sell.
你可以看看我們的目錄。裡頭包括了我們銷售的所有商品。

❹ This **booklet** explains all the details of our construction and assembly processes.
這本小冊子裡頭說明了所有我們的建構和組裝流程的細節。

❺ We give these **pamphlets** to potential buyers at trade shows. They provide the basic facts of our company and products.
我們在商展上提供這些小冊子給潛在消費者。這些小冊子提供了我們公司以及產品的基本資料。

❻ All our products come with a **manual** that clearly explains their usage.
我們所有產品都附上使用手冊，清楚地解說它們的使用方法。

3.5 示範用語 'Demonstration Terms' Language

Show Time

❶ You turn on the motor by **pushing** this **button**.
你按下這個按鈕就可以啓動馬達。

❷ Just **press** the **button** to open the door.
只要壓下這個按鈕就可以把門打開。

❸ Just **turn** this **knob** to open the safe door.
只要轉這個把手就可以開啓安全門。

❹ If you want to open the door, just **turn** the **handle**.
如果你想開門，只要旋轉這個把手即可。

❺ **Grab** this **handle** to carry the box anywhere.
握住這個把手，就可以隨處帶著盒子走。

❻ This **handle** is easy for you to **grasp** when you want to pick it up.
當你想要把它拿起來時，這個把手讓你可以很輕易地握住。

❼ You can turn on the device by **flicking** the **switch**.
只要一開這個開關，就可以啓動這個裝置。

❽ Our scanner is easy to operate. Just **insert** the **plug** into the back of your computer.
我們的掃瞄器很容易操作。只要把插頭插到你的電腦後面即可。

⑨ It is easy to power up. Just **plug** this **plug into** the socket on the wall.

開機很容易。只要把這個插頭插到牆上的插座上即可。

⑩ When you are finished using the product, just **unplug** the **plug**.

當你用完這項產品時,只要把插頭拔掉就可以了。

⑪ Use this key to **lock** the **lock**.

用這個鑰匙把鎖鎖上。

⑫ You can **unlock** the **lock** with this special magnet card.

你可以用這個特殊的磁卡把鎖打開。

⑬ Our shirts use **snaps** instead of buttons. Just **snap** each one with your fingers.

我們的襯衫使用按扣,而不是鈕扣。只要用手指按下每個按扣即可。

⑭ Our coat sleeves have several **buttons** so that you can adjust them yourself. **Button** this one to make it loose, and button this one to make it tight.

我們的大衣的袖子有幾個扣子,這樣你可以自己加以調整。扣住這個就比較鬆,而扣住這個鈕扣就比較緊。

◇◇◇ 小心陷阱 ◇◇◇

☹ 錯誤用法

To turn on the machine, just **pressing** this button.

只要按下這個按鈕就可以啟動這台機器。

☺ 正確用法

To turn on the machine, just **press** this button.

只要按下這個按鈕就可以啟動這台機器。

3.6 說明「產品總類」的用語
'Varieties of Products' Language

Show Time

❶ We have a wonderful **selection** of writing implements.

我們有很棒的精選書寫用具。

❷ Our **line** of cell phone covers is very popular.

我們行動電話話機套的款式非常受歡迎。

❸ The new **version** of our silver necklaces is a little more expensive.

我們新款的銀製項鍊稍微比較貴一些。

❹ We have a wide **range** of colors available for our bathroom towels.

我們的浴室毛巾有各式各樣的顏色。

Word list

implement〔`ɪmpləmənt〕 *n.* 用具；器具

⑤ Our telephones come in many **styles** for both home and office.
我們的電話有許多不同的式樣,適用於家庭以及辦公室。

⑥ There are two **models** of our electric hot plate: small and large.
我們的電熱板有兩款:小的和大的。

⑦ Our **designs** are very fashionable.
我們的設計非常時髦。

⑧ You can choose from one of ten **designs**.
你可以從這十款設計當中挑選。

3.7 「雜項」的用語 'Miscellaneous' Language

Show Time

① Each piece is unique because it is **made by** hand.
每一件都是獨一無二的,因為這是手工製的。

② We would be happy to give you a product **demonstration**.
我們很樂意為您作產品展示。

③ Our mineral water is selling much better than we expected, so we currently have a product **shortage**.
我們的礦泉水賣得比預期理想得多,所以我們目前缺貨。

④ You can increase your order by as much as fifty percent, because we have a **surplus** of the older version.
你可以增加你的訂貨量達百分之五十，因為你訂的舊款我們還有剩。

⑤ We process all our **orders** in twenty-four hours.
我們在二十四小時後處理所有的訂單。

*BIZ*必通片語

❶ **PLACE...ORDER**
下訂單
例 You can **place** an **order** any time by calling our toll-free number.
你可以隨時打我們免付費電話訂貨。
例 Do you want to **place** your **order** today?
你要今天下訂單嗎？

❷ **TAKE...ORDER**
接訂單
例 We can **take** your **order** by phone, fax, or even e-mail.
我們可以電話、傳真、甚至電子郵件接受您的訂單。
例 Can we **take** your **order** now?
我們現在可以接受您的訂貨了嗎？

介紹工廠的字彙
Vocabulary for Talking about the Factory

BIZ必通字彙

工廠各部分 (Parts of the Factory)

❶ assembly line〔ə`sɛmblɪ ,laɪn〕 *n.* 組裝線

❷ line worker〔`laɪn ,wɝkə〕 *n.* 線上工人

❸ machinery〔mə`ʃinərɪ〕 *n.* 機械（總稱）

❹ equipment〔ɪ`kwɪpmənt〕 *n.* 設備

❺ quality control〔`kwɑlətɪ kən`trol〕 *n.* 品質控管

雜項 (Miscellaneous)

❶ automation〔,ɔtə`meʃən〕 *n.* 自動化

❷ production capacity〔prə`dʌkʃən kə`pæsətɪ〕 *n.* 產能

❸ assembly〔ə`sɛmblɪ〕 *n.* 組裝

❹ transportation〔,trænspə`teʃən〕 *n.* 運輸

包裝 (Packaging)

❶ airtight〔`ɛr`taɪt〕 *adj.* 密封的

❷ container〔kən`tenə〕 *n.* 貨櫃；容器

❸ crate〔kret〕 *n.* 板條箱

包裝程序 (Packaging Procedures)

❶ solder〔`sodə〕 *v.* 焊接　　❷ glue〔glu〕 *v.* 粘上

❸ screw〔skru〕 *v.* 旋上　　❹ weld〔wɛld〕 *v.* 熔接

❺ vacuum pack〔`vækjuəm `pæk〕 *v.* 真空包裝

❻ seal〔sil〕 *v.* 密封　　❼ bundle〔`bʌndḷ〕 *v.* 紮；捆

❽ shrink wrap〔`ʃrɪŋk `ræp〕 *v.* 收縮膜包裝

❾ fold〔fold〕 *v.* 摺疊　　❿ assemble〔ə`sɛmbḷ〕 *v.* 組裝

⑪ mold〔mold〕 *v.* 模鑄　　⑫ shape〔ʃep〕 *v.* 塑形
⑬ box up〔bɑks ʌp〕 *v.* 裝箱

4.1 說明「工廠各部分」的用語
'Parts of the Factory' Language

Show Time

❶ The engine components are produced on this **assembly line**.
引擎零件是在這個組裝線生產的。

❷ You can see our **line worker** over there, attaching the metal rods.
你可以看到我們在那兒的生產線員工，他們正在裝上金屬棒。

❸ The **machinery** is all new.
這些機械全部是新的。

❹ All of the **equipment** is cleaned at the end of the day.
一天結束後我們會清洗所有的設備。

❺ This is our **quality control** unit. Right now they are inspecting the latest batch of cookies.
這是我們的品質控制單位。現在他們正在檢查最新出爐的餅乾。

Word list

batch〔bætʃ〕 *n.* 一次出爐的量

┈┈┈┈┈┈┈┈ ◇◇◇ 小心陷阱 ◇◇◇ ┈┈┈┈┈┈┈┈

☹ 錯誤用法

We have four workers on each **assembling** line.

我們每個組裝線有四個工人。

☺ 正確用法

We have four workers on each **assembly** line.

我們每個組裝線有四個工人。

4.2 說明「雜項」的用語 'Miscellaneous' Language

Show Time

❶ Our products require precision assembly, so we have incorporated this new **automation** process.

我們產品需要精準的組裝,所以我們採用了這個新的自動化流程。

❷ The **production capacity** of our Model B-52 is five hundred per week.

我們 B-52 機型的產能是每個禮拜五百個。

❸ You can see that the **assembly** process is very fast.

你可以看到這個組裝流程相當快速。

❹ The **transportation** of all the products in our China factory is provided by Hong Kong Shipping.

我們中國工廠所有產品的運輸都是由香港運輸公司提供的。

4.3 說明「包裝」的用語 'Packaging' Language

Show Time

❶ All of our food products are sealed in **airtight** packages by this machine.
我們所有的食物產品都是用這台機器進行密封包裝。

❷ After the products are packaged, they are put into **containers** for delivery.
產品在包裝之後,便裝入貨櫃中準備運送。

❸ Our trucks transport the **crates** to all parts of Taiwan.
我們的卡車把這些板條箱運到全台灣各地。

4.4 說明「包裝程序」的用語
'Packaging Procedures' Language

Show Time

❶ Our line workers **solder** the pieces together here.
我們生產線的員工在此將這些零件焊接起來。

❷ We use glue guns to **glue** the wooden parts together.
我們用膠槍把這些木製零件黏在一塊。

❸ This machine automatically **screws** the legs into the tables.
這個機器會自動把桌腳旋鎖到桌子上。

❹ In this room our workers **weld** the iron bars.
我們工人在這一間熔接鐵條。

❺ We **vacuum pack** our tea in these packages.
我們把茶葉真空包裝在這些茶葉包裡。

❻ This machine **seals** the lids.
這台機器把蓋子密封起來。

❼ Our workers **bundle** the products into groups of fifteen.
我們的工人把這些產品每十五個紮成一捆。

❽ We **shrink wrap** each package for protection.
我們用收縮膜包裝每包產品作為保護。

❾ In this section we have machines that **fold** each piece into four sections.
在這個部門，我們有機器把每個零件折成四個部分。

❿ The workers at this table **assemble** the pieces into the final product.
這台的工人把零件組裝成最後成品。

⓫ This large machine **molds** the car bodies.
這台大機器模鑄出汽車的車身。

⓬ We have to **shape** each piece so that it resembles a flower.
我們必須把每一片都塑形，好讓它看起來像朵花。

⑬ When the products are ready, we **box** them **up** for immediate shipping.
當產品準備好後，我們會把它們裝箱立刻準備運送。

5 行銷及業務的用語
Marketing & Sales Language

　　記住以下這十個行銷以及業務必通句型。每一家公司都用得上這些用語。你只要把公司的資訊（通常是生產資訊）套用在這些句型內即可。這些句子在西方人聽起來很順耳！（最後一個句子無須代換，只要照說即可）。

BIZ必通句型

❶ **WE MAINLY PRODUCE...**
我們主要生產……
例 We mainly produce steel molds for plastic containers.
我們主要生產塑膠容器的鋼模。

❷ **WE EXPORT OUR PRODUCTS PRIMARILY TO...**
我們的產品主要出口到……
例 We export our products primarily to Europe and East Asia.
我們產品主要出口到歐洲和東亞。

❸ **WE OFFER A WIDE VARIETY OF...**
我們提供各種……
例 We offer a wide variety of sports clothing.
我們提供各種運動服裝。

❹ **OUR SELECTION OF...IS...**
我們精選的……是……
例 Our selection of styles is very large.
我們精選的式樣非常多。

例 Our selection of colors is outstanding.
我們精選的顏色極為出色。

❺ **WE HAVE MANY DIFFERENT...TO CHOOSE FROM.**
我們有各種⋯⋯可以選擇。
例 We have many different models to choose from.
我們有許多不同的機型可供選擇。
例 We have many different sizes to choose from.
我們有許多不同的尺寸可供選擇。

❻ **OUR...RANGE FROM...TO...**
我們的⋯⋯從⋯⋯到⋯⋯都有。
例 Our sizes range from small to extra large.
我們的尺寸從小號到特大號都有。
例 Our lengths range from one meter to three meters.
我們的長度從一公尺到三公尺都有。

❼ **OUR...COME IN...**
我們的⋯⋯有⋯⋯
例 Our blue cases come in many styles.
我們的藍色箱子有許多式樣。
例 Our one liter bottles come in three colors.
我們一公升的瓶子有三種顏色。

❽ **WE PROVIDE THE...THAT YOU WILL FIND IN...**
我們提供⋯⋯（地方）⋯⋯（形容詞＋產品）
例 We provide the best cables that you will find in the world.
我們提供全世界最好的纜線。

例 We provide the most beautiful patterns that you will find in the market.

我們提供市場上最漂亮的圖案。

例 We provide the highest quality tools that you will find in Taiwan.

我們提供台灣最高品質的工具。

❾ WE HAVE BEEN PRODUCING QUALITY...FOR THE LAST...YEARS.

我們過去……年都在生產高品質的……

例 We have been producing quality pens for the last five years.

我們過去五年都是生產高品質的筆。

❿ OUR PRODUCTS ARE THE FINEST QUALITY AVAILABLE.

我們產品的品質是市場上最好的。

Remember the Principles

1 這章的特殊用語可以應用在各種的商業情境上,所以記住這些用語是很實用的。

The special language presented in this chapter can be used for all kinds of business situations, so it is very useful to remember the language.

2 仔細地看這些範例以了解如何運用每個字彙。

Examine the examples carefully so that you will understand how to use each vocabulary word.

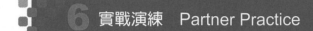

6 實戰演練 Partner Practice

依據下列情境，找個同伴一起模擬對話，作為實戰前的演練。

① A是台灣人，B是外國人。雙方都在A的辦公室（扮演A的人可以設想真的在自己的辦公室）。
  1) B：詢問洗手間在哪裡
     A：說明洗手間的位置
  2) B：詢問洗手間的方向
     A：指引洗手間的方向
  3) B：詢問（某個東西）的位置
     A：說明位置
  4) B：詢問（某個東西）的方向
     A：指引方向

② A是台灣人，B是外國人。他們正在討論A的產品（討論實際的產品）
  1) A：說明產品細節
     B：詢問更多細節的問題
  2) A：展示產品的使用
     B：詢問更多細節的問題

③ 這個情境當中，只要扮演自己就可以了！如果可能的話，帶領B參觀你的公司和你的工廠。A談論公司和生產流程的細節。B則詢問問題，要求A進一步加以說明、提供更多的細節並釐清不清楚的地方。

國家圖書館出版品預行編目資料

搞定商務口說 / Dana Forsythe 作；胡瑋珊譯. －－
　初版. －－臺北市；貝塔語言，2003〔民92〕
　　面；　　公分
　中英對照
　ISBN 957-729-293-3（平裝附光碟片）

　1. 商業英語－會話

805.188　　　　　　　　　　　　　　91022873

搞定商務口說
Oral Business Communication

作　　者 / Dana Forsythe
總 編 審 / 王復國
譯　　者 / 胡瑋珊
執行編輯 / 陳家仁

出　　版 / 貝塔語言出版有限公司
地　　址 / 台北市 100 館前路 12 號 11 樓
電　　話 / (02)2314-2525
傳　　真 / (02)2312-3535
郵　　撥 / 19493777 貝塔出版有限公司
客服專線 / (02)2314-3535
客服信箱 / btservice@betamedia.com.tw

總 經 銷 / 時報文化出版企業股份有限公司
地　　址 / 桃園縣龜山鄉萬壽路二段 351 號
電　　話 / (02) 2306-6842

出版日期 / 2005 年 9 月初版四刷
定　　價 / 350 元
ISBN：957-729-293-3

Oral Business Communication
Copyright 2003 by Dana Forsythe
Published by Beta Multimedia Publishing
The people, places, companies, organizations or events mentioned in the sample
sentences and/or articles in this book are for learning purposes only and do not
depict real or actual people, places, companies, organizations or events.

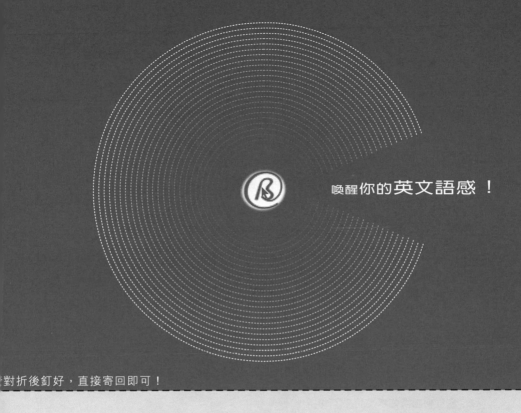

喚醒你的英文語感 ！

對折後釘好，直接寄回即可！

| 廣 告 回 信 |
| 北區郵政管理局登記證 |
| 北 台 字 第 1 4 2 5 6 號 |
| 免 貼 郵 票 |

100 台北市中正區館前路12號11樓

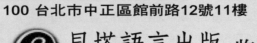

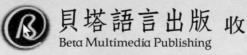

貝塔語言出版 收
Beta Multimedia Publishing

寄件者住址 □ □ □

![Beta logo] 貝塔語言出版
Beta Multimedia Publishing

讀者服務專線（02）2314-3535　　讀者服務傳真（02）2312-3535
客戶服務信箱 btservice@betamedia.com.tw

www.betamedia.com.tw

謝謝您購買本書！！

貝塔語言擁有最優良之英文學習書籍，為提供您最佳的英語學習資訊，您可填妥此表後寄回（免貼郵票）或至http://www.betamedia.com.tw登錄為貝塔書友，您將不定期免費收到本公司最新發行書訊及活動訊息！

姓名：＿＿＿＿＿＿＿＿＿＿＿＿　性別：□男 □女　生日：＿＿＿年＿＿＿月＿＿＿日
電話：(公)＿＿＿＿＿＿＿＿＿＿(宅)＿＿＿＿＿＿＿＿＿＿(手機)＿＿＿＿＿＿＿＿＿
學歷：□高中職含以下 □專科 □大學 □研究所含以上
職業：□金融 □服務 □傳播 □製造 □資訊 □軍公教 □出版
　　　□自由 □教育 □學生 □其他
職級：□企業負責人 □高階主管 □中階主管 □職員 □專業人士

1. 您購買的書籍是？＿＿＿＿＿＿＿＿＿＿＿＿＿＿＿＿＿＿＿＿＿＿
2. 您從何處得知本產品？(可複選)
　　　□書店 □網路 □書展 □校園活動 □廣告信函 □他人推薦 □新聞報導 □其他
3. 您覺得本產品價格：
　　　□偏高 □合理 □偏低
4. 請問目前您每週花了多少時間學英語？
　　　□ 不到十分鐘 □ 十分鐘以上，但不到半小時 □ 半小時以上，但不到一小時
　　　□ 一小時以上，但不到兩小時 □ 兩個小時以上 □ 不一定
5. 通常在選擇語言學習書時，哪些因素是您會考慮的？
　　　□ 封面 □ 內容、實用性 □ 品牌 □ 媒體、朋友推薦 □ 價格□ 其他＿＿＿＿＿
6. 市面上您最需要的語言書種類為？
　　　□ 聽力 □ 閱讀 □ 文法 □ 口說 □ 寫作 □ 其他＿＿＿＿＿＿
7. 通常您會透過何種方式選購語言學習書籍？
　　　□ 書店門市 □ 網路書店 □ 郵購 □ 直接找出版社 □ 學校或公司團購
　　　□ 其他＿＿＿＿＿＿＿
8. 給我們的建議：＿＿＿＿＿＿＿＿＿＿＿＿＿＿＿＿＿＿＿＿＿＿＿＿＿
＿＿＿＿＿＿＿＿＿＿＿＿＿＿＿＿＿＿＿＿＿＿＿＿＿＿＿＿＿＿＿＿＿